MASTERSON UNLEASHED

Masterson Series Book Two

LISA LANG BLAKENEY

Writergirl Press

LISA LANG BLAKENEY
Love reading novels featuring hot alpha men who fall for smart women?
Then join <u>MY VIP MAILING LIST</u> at http://LisaLangBlakeney.
com/VIP and get a free book just for joining!

FOLLOW ME
Follow me on Facebook
Join my Fan Group
Follow me on Amazon
Follow me on Bookbub
Follow me on Instagram

License Note

This book is a work of fiction. Any similarity to real events, people, or places is entirely coincidental. All rights reserved. This book may not be reproduced or distributed in any format without the permission of the author, except in the case of brief quotations used for review.

The author acknowledges the trademarked status of products referred to in this book and acknowledges that trademarks have been used without permission.

This book contains mature content, including graphic sex. Please do not continue reading if you are under the age of 18 or if this type of content is disturbing to you.

NOTE: All characters in the book are 18+ years of age, non-blood related, and all sexual acts are consensual.

What Readers Are Saying About Lisa

"Lisa writes books that are intense. Explosive. Panty Melting. Raw. Exposed. Angst. Multifaceted."

"Cover to cover, page by page every word was amazing. This author is amazing and her work is even more amazing. She really can get all the details and words to sound great together."

"As soon as I picked up book 1 I was addicted to this series. I couldn't wait for this one to come out!"

"I definitely recommend this series to readers. It was the first of its kind that I have read, and I was not disappointed. 5 Stars!"

To Mommy

Books By Lisa

The Masterson Series

Devour this addictive series about the possessive bad boy, Roman Masterson, who falls hard and fast for the girl he's promised his family to protect.

Masterson

Masterson Unleashed

Masterson In Love

Masterson Made

Joseph Loves Juliette

Masterson Box Set

Masterson Next Generation Series

The crazy hot fruit doesn't fall far from the tree. Dive into this second generation of Masterson men!

Knox - Knox & Gigi

Bronx - Bronx & Karma

Seven - Coming soon!

The King Brothers Series

Dive into this series of interconnected standalones featuring 3 alpha hot brothers and the women they lay claim to without apology.

Claimed - Camden & Jade

Indebted - Cutter & Sloan

Broken - Stone & Tiny

Promised - All King Brothers

King Brothers Box Set

The Nighthawk Series

Sexy & sweet sports romances set in the professional world of football. All standalones.

Saint - Saint & Sabrina

Wolf - Cooper & Ursula

Diesel - Mason & Olivia

Jett - Jett & Adrienne

Rush - Rush & Mia

Freak - Freak & Willow

Brick - coming soon!

Introduction

I made a mistake and had a taste of something sweet, something forbidden, something highly addictive...Elizabeth. It's no secret that I'm greedy, and I want more. Now I just have to convince her pretty ass that she does too.

Just as things begin to heat up between Elizabeth and Roman, she pulls away frightened of what it all means and goes off to pursue funding for her new business.

Convincing people to make decisions that they wouldn't normally make is Roman's specialty. It's just that he's going to have to find other more creative ways to make this particular target bend to his will.

Please note that this book was previously published under the title of Cousins Book Two.

Roman

"WHAT THE HELL is wrong with you?"

I should notice Jade in the room, because she's basically standing directly in front of me with her legs shoulder width apart, both hands on her hips, and her miniature skull cocked to the side; but I'm so inside of my own head right now, it's almost as if she's a silhouette blending into the background with the rest of the furniture.

I should also probably hear everything Jade is saying to me, because she's popping her usual wad of god-awful gum in her mouth while talking completely at me, but even her voice is like white noise to me right now.

I don't hear shit.

I'm sitting on the floor of my living room, methodically taking apart and reassembling my Beretta 92FS while separating and scarfing down yellow peanut M&Ms. If a stranger was a fly on the wall inside my apartment right now, he or she would probably be staring at me as if I was completely certifiable; basically how Jade is looking at me at this very minute.

What I've never told her or anyone for that matter is

that I was taught by a school counselor, who I was forced to meet with in the twelfth grade (by Joseph's request I suspect), that I needed to create rituals for myself in order to self soothe.

In other words, to calm the fuck down.

When my insides are dark and stormy, this is what I do. I either create a new ritual on the fly or fall back on one of my old standards, but whichever method I select, they always have to mean something to me. And only me.

I was barely six years old when my mother woke me up on a weekday at five a.m. and announced that we were going to walk all the way from our house to Walmart (which was at least two miles away) and wait for them to open. She had purchased a vacuum cleaner from there that she wanted to return immediately, because the power cord would not automatically wind back inside its compartment, and she was livid. This is what it could be like living with my mother. She acted on every impulse, every whim, and every emotion. Many times at my expense.

After the time it took to get there, we waited another two hours for Walmart to open that day, and then she told me to sit on the walkway in front of the store with the vacuum cleaner while she made a run to the bank. I didn't understand at my age that there were no banks open at seven a.m., at least not in our neighborhood, so I did as I was told and waited.

It was cold that day and the longer I sat on the concrete, and the longer she was gone, the more anxious I became. I was shivering with my arms around a vacuum cleaner box as store employees pulled inside the parking lot to begin their workday. Most of them gave me inquisitive but brief glances as they continued their labored marches inside the building. Everyone except a cashier named Caroline. A round, robust woman with little to no hair on her head (my guess was due to chemo) but a huge smile, and she stopped to speak to me when no one else bothered to that day.

"Why are you sitting out here all alone son?"

"My mom's vacuum cleaner doesn't work."

"Where is your momma?"

"At the bank."

"The bank? Which one?"

"I don't know."

"Hmmm … what's your name?"

"Roman. What's yours?"

"See my name tag? Can you read it?"

"Yep. It says Caroleene."

"That's Caroline."

"That's what I said. Caroleene."

She flashed me another one of her warm smiles.

"Are you in school yet, Roman?"

"Sometimes." I said not realizing what was very wrong with that answer.

"You want to come inside with the vacuum cleaner and wait for your momma there, Roman? It's chilly out here, and you'll get hemor-rhoids if you stay sittin' on that concrete."

I liked the looks of Caroline. Even though she was missing a lot of hair, she still looked kind and fluffy like someone's grandma should look. But I could hear my mother's voice in my head, warning me to avoid all strangers, especially kind ones. My mom didn't trust many people and even when I really wanted to, I didn't either.

"I'll wait for my mommy out here."

"Fair enough, but here's a little something while you wait. Free of charge."

Caroline smiled when she handed me a small unopened bag of M&Ms. It was the first time I had candy since I could remember, and even though I had been warned about accepting food, gifts, or kindness from strangers, I made an exception that morning.

"It's my only guilty pleasure. I have plenty more at home unfortunately. You take these," she offered.

"Thank you." I said as I ripped the bag open almost immediately. Not realizing how hungry I was.

"What good manners, and you're welcome darlin'. But listen, Roman, make sure to eat each one of those candies one by one and very slowly. It will help pass the time until your mom gets back. Okay?"

"Okay."

"You promise?"

"I promise."

Time passed longer than I ever anticipated that day and now that I'm older and wiser, it's obvious that sweet, old Miss Caroline figured that it was going to be a long morning for me. It was the first time that my mother had ever left me somewhere and then completely forgot about me. She usually came back within at least an hour.

This time she didn't.

I was still sitting outside Walmart three hours later, when the tears started to roll down my face and the realization hit me that my mother wasn't coming back for me. I knew then that I had a decision to make. Should I try and look for my mother? Should I try and make my way back home? Or should I go inside and ask that sweet old woman for help?

I ate the last of my M&Ms while I thought things through and was able to arrive at my first of many future big boy decisions. I was going to figure out my way back home, with the vacuum cleaner in tow, and hoped that my mother would remember her way back home too.

Almost five hours later she did.

· · ·

I'm lining up the peanut version of my favorite candy side by side on my smoked glass coffee table, then eating only the yellow ones. Eating M&Ms to calm myself down is one of my go to rituals thanks to the kind woman I met many years ago. Making it yellow M&Ms is something I'm doing on the fly. Something that reminds me of the very person that has my insides all twisted in knots. Yellow is Elizabeth's favorite color.

And she's all I can think about.

Her mouth.

Her breasts.

Her laugh.

That spectacular ass.

I don't especially like that images of her are creeping around inside of my head, consuming my thoughts, but the fact remains that I brought all this shit on myself once I put my hands and mouth on her and especially my damn dick inside of her. I have no one to blame but my fucking self.

It's like a switch has been flipped on inside of me that I couldn't power off even if I wanted to. What I think I hate most about how I'm feeling is that it's all so new and foreign to me. This desire to always know where she's at, what she's doing, and how she's feeling is actually a big pain in my ass. That shit is for weak pussies. Not for men like me.

My old school counselor would probably say I'm having an issue, because I don't know how to interpret and control unfamiliar emotional responses or some such nonsensical shit. She was right about one thing though. I do like control. I definitely like knowing exactly what I'm dealing with at all times. I don't like surprises, and I don't like chaos. And while I'm sure it's no big deal in many circles that I have hooked up with a family member who is only my cousin by marriage, in my world it's a big fucking deal.

It's messy.

None of my friends or family would ever understand this. In our world, she's still very much family. They'd probably come up with many creative names for what I am: perverted, distorted, warped, depraved, pathetic. I know this because I would probably think the same thing.

Problem is right now … I just don't give a fuck.

And the only reason why I've been holding back as much as I have with Elizabeth is because I know that she definitely does give a fuck.

I've swallowed four Extra-Strength Excedrin and drank at least three highballs of Jack Daniels over the last hour, but my head is still fucking pounding and my gut is still wickedly churning. Probably because over the last twenty-four hours the same questions have been running through my head, gnawing at me.

What is Elizabeth doing? Who is she talking to? Why hasn't she returned my texts or calls? Is she okay? Has that prick Ethan slick-talked himself in between her legs right now? Does Joseph have enough pull to be able to bail my ass out if I kill a motherfucker in the Bahamas?

I'm checking and cleaning the slide and barrel of my gun for the third time now, because it's one of my rituals, and also because I really want to figure out a seriously creative way to transport an unregistered gun across international waters and into Paradise Island.

I'm not fucking playing.

It's a good thing federal laws are in place to prevent me from actually acting on it. Of course no law will stop me from breaking Ethan's jaw. I am already pissed that Elizabeth left the country without even as much as a good-bye to me, but now that Jade told me that Elizabeth's ex-boyfriend could possibly be in the exact same place, I've moved into I want to kick someone's ass mode. I want to break some shit the fuck up.

I just have to be very careful about how I approach this. No one can know just how twisted up I am. I'm going to have to rein my crazy in, or it's going to look like I'm going ape-shit over my cousin, which I am, but that's besides the point.

"Earth to Roman." Jade speaks to me with the tone of a perturbed elementary school teacher as she taps me on the forehead. "I asked what the hell is wrong with you?"

"Why are you still here, Jade?" For a minute I forgot she was even in my house.

"I literally just told you that your cousin who's over a thousand miles away may be in some trouble. I've watched you zone out on me, play with your gun, and eat more yellow M&Ms than any one person should be allowed to over the last few minutes. What gives? You should be going all bad ass right about now. Calling in the troops. Making shit happen."

"All I said was research her ex for me. I never said that she was in any trouble."

Jade looks at me incredulously. I can't even blame her. I sound like a complete liar.

"Are you freaking kidding me? You didn't have to say it. It's a given that if we're looking into someone that they may be a problem. And all I just said to you was that the Ethan kid may be in the Bahamas, and now you look like you want to kill somebody. I mean look at you. What don't I know? Why did you trash your apartment, and why are you acting like a complete nut-ball right now?"

"I didn't want–" I stop myself from saying the words.

"You didn't what?"

I grunt and shake my head no, so that Jade will shut

the fuck up, but she isn't the type to take a hint. She's like a tiny little Chihuahua that latches on and doesn't let go until she gets what she came for. Blood.

"I don't know."

"I've known you a long time, Roman, and I've never seen you like this. So agitated. So indecisive. You do realize that there's no room in your world for whatever this is that you're going through? There are no days off for you."

"I know that Jade," I say with tension in my voice. I'm ten seconds away from pinging a yellow M&M at her annoying little head. They're both about the same size.

"I'm not indecisive about shit, Jade. Elizabeth's a big girl. If she decides to hook back up with her ex in the Bahamas then that's her business. She'll call home if there's any trouble."

Jade gives me a lengthy sidelong glance.

"Is that what this is about? You're mad that she may be hooking back up with the ex?"

I turn my head and glare hard at Jade. I already know that she knows about my unhealthy attraction towards Elizabeth, because of how I was acting at the club, but saying that shit out loud is a whole other matter.

"Don't give me the stink eye, boss man. I get it. I had a crush on one of my cousins when I was in high school and had no problem letting the whole entire family know about it either. I used to follow him all over the house during family dinners like a little puppy dog, but being attracted to your cousin is just like having the hots for your best friend's boyfriend. It's completely fine and totally normal as long as you don't act on it; and you haven't acted on it right?"

I don't answer Jade, because I know that she means that as a rhetorical question. One that she wouldn't like the honest answer to. She takes my silence and my blank face to mean that I haven't crossed any lines yet and continues on with her spiel.

"I don't see how you can just sit here playing with guns and scarfing down candy knowing that her douchebag ex may be knocking on her hotel room door right this minute. You asked me to look into him and I did. I know he has some drug issues, and Elizabeth doesn't seem the type to tolerate someone like that. So why aren't you doing anything about it? Imagine Joseph's reaction if something does happen to her, while you sit here paralyzed with some sort of misplaced guilt. What a fixer."

Okay now her sarcastic ass is fucking pushing it.

"Watch it, Jade." I growl.

"Do you want me to book your ticket to the island or not?"

Of course I do.

That little fucker is there.

I can feel it.

Once Jade said the words, I knew right then and there that it was true. And if he's there, he could only be there for Elizabeth. There's no fucking way it's a coincidence. I know sneaky, lying drug addicts. I grew up with and around a shit load of them, and he is definitely one. He just goes to fancier schools and dresses better.

I lock the magazine clip of my gun into the receiver for the final time, lay my piece down on the table with a quiet thump, and swallow my last yellow M&M. I'm the hell done with self-soothing. I work better with an edge to me any fucking way.

"Book me a one-way ticket to Nassau and a room at the Atlantis."

I practically roll my eyes at the smirk that spreads across Jade's face. She loves it when she wins.

"How do you know she's staying there?"

"Juliette mentioned it."

"So you want one of the penthouse suites?"

I usually get the best that my money can buy when I travel, but not this time.

"No. Find out what tower she's staying in and book me the best room they have on her floor. It has to be on the same floor."

"What about Joseph and the Kings?"

"It's none of their business."

"You are working cases right now Roman. You've got the clubs too. You're going to have to say something to them."

She's right as usual. That's why I have Jade around. She gives me shit, and drives me crazy, but she keeps me on point. She knows my business is everything to me. It's all I really have that matters.

"Joseph and Juliette know that she's in the Bahamas on business, so there's no point in telling them anything different. I'll have Cutter cover the clubs and Camden can work the DUI job. Just tell Cam and Cutter the truth. Tell them that Elizabeth may be in some trouble, and that I have to go out of town to handle it. Play it down though. No red alerts. No telling the old man that I went there. You feel me?"

Jade nods with satisfaction. "I'm glad you've finally come to your senses. While I know that it's possible that Elizabeth may be sitting on a beach, catching a tan, and reading a novel, there's also the small chance that this Ethan guy is up to something. Once upon a time you helped me out of a messed up situation that nobody gave a shit about, and I just think that someone should have Elizabeth's back too."

"Understood."

"What about killer over there?"

Jade points over to the corner at Mr. Tibbs. Jade is not a dog person. Usually I have someone house sit him if I travel, but this is too last minute. Plus I like giving Jade shit sometimes.

It completes me.

"Raw chicken backs and turkey necks are portioned in Ziploc bags in the freezer. Feed him twice a day. No treats. He also gets three walks a day. And clean this place up and water my plant while you're at it. Juliette gave it to me."

"I'm not touching any raw chicken backs or turkey necks! I swear that damn dog is going to starve."

I walk away grinning like a Cheshire cat as I hear Jade's cries of protest behind me. It's a pleasure to piss her off as I head to my bedroom to pack, and go see about kicking some ass in order to bring my cousin home where she belongs.

2

Elizabeth

ALL I HEAR ARE PIERCING squeals of joy.

Rolling laughter.

Playful shrieking.

These are all sounds that are probably delightful to a mother's ears, but are like nails across a chalkboard to my delicate, twenty-three year old ones. But that's okay, because if you told me last week that I'd be snacking on the freshest shrimp cocktail of my life while watching families of four sliding down a massive water slide into a crystal blue manmade lagoon, I would have never believed it.

The only place my family has ever vacationed is Disney World, and that was a big damn deal. My parents would save up all year, and we'd go with my mom's best friend Miss Janet and her two monsters (I mean kids) and end up lost, hot, and exhausted most days. No squealing. No shrieking. Minimal laughter. As my parents often complained, "Disney World was a week of work and not a true vacation."

They were right; it probably was work for them, not to mention disappointing for me, because they'd never buy me a new Disney Princess dress as a souvenir. Just a pair of Minnie Mouse ears. And how many pairs of those does a girl need?

But this right here, this whole Bahamas thing is what I've always imagined vacations were supposed to be. Relaxing. Fun. Lush. Serene. Good food. Fruity drinks. Surrounded by beautiful people.

It probably helps that Mr. Lambert and his team have treated me extremely well, especially for someone only here to give them a fifteen minute pitch. They flew me non-stop for three hours in business class to Nassau, Bahamas, then I was picked up by a car service and taken to the hotel, where I was checked in immediately to the most beautiful room with an ocean view.

The only thing I'm not really happy about is that I'm literally two minutes away from Florida, but my cell phone service is spotty at best. It's almost like I'm in some sort of third world country with no cell phone towers, when it's obvious I'm not. While beautiful in places, the Bahamas is definitely not some untouched island. It's actually like one huge city with a few pretty beaches.

So if I wanted to, I could cross the street and order a six piece Chicken Mcnugget and fries; and in my opinion if there is a damn McDonald's nearby then there certainly needs to be reliable cell phone service. When I get home I'm going to have to have a long talk with my phone carrier.

Luckily for me, I'm only here for a day or so, so being out of touch is not such a big deal. I've already called my Aunt Juliette and my mom from my room to let them know that I've arrived safely, and that I have an amazing view. Of course Juliette offered to upgrade my room to an Azure or Sapphire Suite, which I politely declined. My deluxe oceanfront view is fantastic already. Anything more would be overkill.

My two calls back home will be charged to my final bill, which I can cover at checkout with a credit card, but I need to cut myself off there. No more international calls. No more frivolous spending unless I nail this pitch and get a definite yes. I would have liked to talk to Sloan for a second though, because she is totally responsible for setting this meeting up, but I know that she'll understand if I just connect with her when I touch back down in Philly.

I also thought about sending Roman an email to let him know where I was going (actually I thought about it like fifty-five hundred times), but I'm pretty sure that Juliette and Joseph filled him in on my trip. And after I practically ran away from his apartment like I had been set on fire, I'm sure he's quite annoyed with me or even worse— pissed with me. Actually I'm a bit peeved with myself. There's no excuse for my behavior. I'm sending him some seriously mixed signals and driving myself bonkers in the process.

When I was over his penthouse the other day, I let Roman do things to me that I've only heard Sloan talk about or read in smutty books, and while I loved every minute of it, I was extremely embarrassed afterwards. I just can't wrap my head around it. Why I acted like I did. I never tried to stop him once or even tried to stop myself. What's wrong with me?

The minute I hear the bass in his voice, I immediately become wet like a faucet and proceed to pop my legs open for easy access. And the orgasms? Geez Louise. I thought I was going to pass out from the intense contractions and spasms my poor uterus and vagina had to weather. Okay maybe the use of the word poor is not exactly accurate. I think my lady parts liked every frackin' minute of it.

This attraction Roman and I have for each other is almost cruel though. As soon as he started telling me what he was going to do, my body responded in turn. The way my body almost sings when he strokes every part of me, it's like my body desperately needs him. In fact I do believe that my body is starting to crave more of his touch everyday. Hell, my body is missing him right the frack now. But of course the cruel part of all of this is why him? Why couldn't it be anybody else but Roman Masterson ... my cousin?

If our families were to ever find out what's been going on between the two of us, I shudder to think of the harsh words that would inevitably pass between my father's lips to my aunt and her husband. He already despises Joseph for some ridiculous reason that I don't even being to understand; so this thing between Roman and I would just be the kindling he needs to start an all out forest fire. And that's the last thing I want. I don't want to be the cause of any sort of family civil war.

Especially when I know better.

Especially because I know this is wrong.

I just need to grow the hell up and stop spreading my legs for every sexy thing he says in my ear, and for every kiss he barely gives me right at the corner of my lips, and for all the times he's stared at me like I was the only woman breathing on the planet.

Damn.

After filling my belly with the rest of my shrimp cocktail and a frosted glass of fruit punch, I head back to my room in order to shower and change. Mr. Lambert breaks for forty-five minutes between his two panels, and I only have an hour before that happens. I've been told that I'll have his full attention in the Poseidon meeting room during the first fifteen minutes of that break. My mouth is a little dry and my nerves a bit frayed in anticipation, but all in all, I think that I'm as ready as I'll ever be to deliver my pitch.

I went over my presentation with a fine-tooth comb during the plane ride, and that's why I purposely turned off my computer when I landed. I didn't want to burn myself out or change anything at the last minute in a moment of anxiety or fear. I need to trust that I know what I'm doing, and that I know what I'm talking about, and that these men will have the foresight to see the tremendous potential of my app.

A short ding signaling that I have a text comes in from Mr. Lambert's assistant Daniella finalizing the time that I should come down to the conference room.

Daniella: Please be at the Poseidon room at 3:15 sharp Miss Hill. Mr. Lambert and the rest of the group will be assembled and waiting.

Me: Thank you. I'll be there.

A small knot forms in my chest.

I'm definitely nervous.

No matter how much I try to psyche myself out of becoming a stressed out mess, it's inevitable; I'm a hormonal wreck. I do the math in my head and figure out that my period is coming on soon. On top of everything else, that may be adding to my crazy.

I strip myself bare and stare at myself in the mirror. My hair is wind blown and my skin sun kissed from sitting by the lagoon all morning. Not bad. All totally fixable. I stare further down and notice a small mole has popped up in between my breasts. It's new. I wonder what it would cost to get it removed. I gaze even lower and wonder for the hundredth time if I should get a Brazilian wax. A couple of girls from my old job at The Tavern used to rave about them.

"You'll be smooth as a baby's bottom, Elizabeth. Your man will love it." They'd say.

Little did they realize that the term smooth as a baby's bottom turned me completely off from the whole thing. I didn't want to sleep with a man who wanted a woman's snatch to be as smooth as a prepubescent girl's. Of course I've occasionally had second thoughts about this every time I take a good look at my private parts. Vaginas aren't necessarily pretty in my opinion, especially mine, because it's totally covered with a lot of wiry and unruly hair just like the top of my head.

After shutting down all my negative thoughts and giving my body a more positive final once over, I'm ready to get showered and dressed.

You're not sleeping with any of these men Elizabeth.

You're pitching an app that could basically sell itself.

You've got this.

Yellow is my lucky color. I've loved it since way back, probably influenced by the many spring days I spent collecting buttercups and dandelions in my backyard as a kid. But I learned that it was good luck for sure when I wore my lucky yellow shirt on Black and Gold Day in middle school.

It was that day the Gold team (which I was on) finally kicked the Black team's butt in flag football, when it had been the Black team that had won the title for the last four years. It was also the same day that the nicest boy in seventh grade, Matt Kellum, noticed that I was alive and breathing. I fell while running with the flag, and when he helped me up he told me "Good job Hill". It was one of my fondest memories of middle school. I didn't even realize that he knew my name … or that I even existed.

So I'm waffling between wearing a navy blue power suit with a pale yellow tank underneath the jacket, or wearing a dark gray pencil skirt with a scoop neck lemon yellow blouse. The suit means business. The skirt accentuates the shape of my wide hips. Something men seem to like on me no matter how much I vehemently disagree.

I was meeting with a room full of men.

Some of them really close to my age.

The skirt wins.

Turns out that I made the right decision, because I'm sitting around an oblong conference table full of men. Most of whom are under forty years old. I recognize immediately the guy that Sloan is connected to, because while we were never formally introduced, I've seen pictures of him in several of Sloan's Instagram selfies.

Due to nerves, I'm tempted to twirl around in the plush, ergonomic chair I'm sitting in, but think better of it once Mr. Lambert enters the room.

"It's a pleasure, Miss Hill."

Mr. Lambert extends his hand to shake mine. I stand up to do the same knowing that a few eyeballs in the room have instantly landed on my ass.

"The pleasure is mine, Mr. Lambert." I turn my head and smile. "Gentlemen."

"So you have our attention, Miss Hill. Let's hear about School Bucks."

I can feel a trickle of sweat rolling down my back, while the room is as cold as a Chicago winter. I am obviously still nervous. To talk myself off the ledge, I begin to silently go through everything Sloan told me about the men in the group.

She mentioned that they were smart and selective, but that they were also very motivated in getting into tech investments, and definitely highly motivated in investing in new female entrepreneurs. Something about certain funds they managed that were earmarked for female business owners.

She instructed me to look every single man there in the eye during my presentation but to end it looking at Mr. Lambert. Something about it being the art of the close. Sloan also stressed that I needed to walk around the room while I talked. She said that many of them would be distracted by my body and focused on my movements, which was a good thing. In my opinion, it's bad enough that I'm wearing the pencil skirt (that if I'm honest is one size too small), but to walk around in it purposely to showcase my ass seems a little sexist and screams of desperation.

Of course that doesn't mean that I'm not going to do it.

I do.

After a brief description of my app, I stand up and decide to walk around the table as I hand out a printed copy of my presentation to each and every member of the group. There are eight men in total. A few are smiling at me while I talk (including Sloan's guy), a few are reading the materials I hand out while I am talking, and Mr. Lambert is copiously taking notes on a yellow legal pad.

Seems to be a good sign.

I make sure to complete my presentation in ten minutes flat, so that I have five minutes for any quick questions and answers. There are several.

The first is from an intimidating man with a set of unforgettable bushy eyebrows named Ned Harrison. He looks like my old professor from my statistics class.

"So you majored in computer engineering and minored in information systems, but you're not the coder of the app. Is that right?"

I clear my throat nervously.

"I'm the architect, but I needed more experienced coders to construct the app and to tweak and test the fine details. Moving forward, I'd definitely want someone on board who has the skills to update the app as needed. Every time Apple or Android comes out with a new operating system, we have to update the app. And we'd probably be updating it more often than that as we build out the database."

Ned Harrison nods his head at my answer but doesn't look at me any longer. That worries me. The second question is from a man named Bob Hathaway.

"This was a well thought out presentation Miss Hill, but I have to be honest here, there is no fiscal sense in us investing in one product. Do you have any sort of long term plan of expansion? What other apps could you roll out that would be in alignment with this one?"

A good question. One that I don't have a really good answer for or at least an answer that he wants. I'll have to bullshit.

"Absolutely. There are several app ideas I have that are in the planning stages."

Uh ... and what the frack are they Elizabeth?

"To be honest, I'm still working out the details of those apps and would rather not divulge any particulars. Be assured though that they are congruent with the overall mission of my business, which is to support the average American student's quest in forming a viable plan to finance their higher education. The average college student has many financial needs for over four to eight years, and my applications are designed to support those needs."

I pray that my bullshit worked on at least half the men at this table. After I'm done talking, I notice a few head nods around the table and a few more notes taken by Mr.

Lambert, and then just like that my first and only pitch meeting is over.

"Well thank you so much, Miss Hill. You've given us a lot to consider."

Hmm … maybe this didn't go so well. I've heard of investors so excited that they made offers right in the middle of a pitch. Sort of like that show Shark Tank, but I understand, I'm new and unproven. Plus I'm young, and I don't actually do the coding. They have to take all of that into consideration.

At worst I received a free trip to the Bahamas out of the deal. In fact, I'm going to make this trip even better by heading to the bar right now.

"Thank you gentlemen and thank you for the extraordinary hospitality. I look forward to hearing from you in the near future. Please feel free to contact me with any further questions."

A few of the men stand up as I make my way to the door including Mr. Lambert. He walks with me outside of the conference room and into the hallway.

"You did really well, Miss Hill. Daniella will be in touch with you, although I can't guarantee exactly when. We have a lot of offers to consider and limited funds. In the meantime, do what you can to increase the app's visibility and profitability, and send over any new figures if that happens."

"Thank you, Mr. Lambert. Really. I appreciate everything that you've done for me. Giving me this chance."

"You're welcome, Miss Hill."

I need wine.

Sangria to be specific.

There are several restaurants and one main bar on my side of the hotel. I don't really want anything to eat, but I definitely could use a drink to drown out the constant replay of the pitch meeting in my head.

Either I have the strong makings of becoming a drunk, or a thing for bartenders because I like them. I like talking to them, watching them pour a drink, wondering who they are outside of work. It's weird I know. The bartender I'm stalking tonight is nothing like the guy from The Lotus (Marco). This guy is extra tall and somewhat hard looking with beautiful cocoa brown skin and blood-shot eyes.

"Would you like to order?" he asks with what I assume is a heavy Bahamian accent.

"What's better?" I smile. "The white or red sangria?"

"The red," he replies without a smile in return.

"I'll have an extra big glass of that." I say in an effort to exaggerate just how much I need it right now. And that gets me a small lift at the corner of his lips.

"Coming up."

After gulping down an entire glass of the best sangria I've ever had in my life, I'm still in replay mode. Maybe I should have stressed the low overhead. How could I have forgotten to include potential other apps in the presentation? Perhaps I should have worn the power suit.

Hell, I could second guess this all night. I need to face the facts that there isn't much I can do about it now. The meeting is over. The best I can do is follow up with a thank you letter reiterating my greatness blah, blah, blah.

The bartender with little words walks back over to check on me.

"Another?" he asks.

I need to remember my budget.

"How much are they?" I ask a little embarrassed.

And then I hear a voice from the end of the bar that I haven't heard in what seems like a lifetime.

"I've got her next drink."

Oh my frackin' God.

"Ethan?"

3

Roman

I'VE BEEN SITTING IN my father's home office for at least twenty-five minutes and my brain is like a ticking time bomb, about to explode, but of course I would never reveal that to Joseph. I never have and I never will reveal all my crazy to him.

Unfortunately he caught me on my way to the airport, so I had to swing by and at least show my face for a few minutes.

"We need to talk about Mendez." My father growls while angrily typing an email at his desk. "Dammit, I can't find any of my emails in this new layout. Why do they keep changing everything? By the time you learn it, they go and change it."

I could care less about the old man's inability to stay current with technology, and I don't care about Mendez either. In fact, I don't want to talk about any business shit with Joseph period. All I want to do is get to the motherfucking airport.

I take a few deep internal breaths. I can't lose it in front of the old man. I just need to handle this calmly. Rationally. Quickly. I can't set off any alarms.

Control your shit, Masterson.

"What about Mendez?" I ask casually while I grab a few M&Ms out of the small bag in my pocket and toss them in my mouth.

Joseph looks up from his computer and watches me closely for a moment.

"What's wrong with you?" he asks after a long pause.

"Nothing."

I'm caught off guard by the question, because frankly I thought that I had been keeping my need for the M&M ritual on the low all my life. In fact most people think it is a sign of my calm confidence in a stressful situation when I eat them, when actually it is the complete opposite.

But I suppose that just because Joseph isn't a warm and fuzzy father, doesn't mean that he doesn't know me. He definitely knows something is up, but I'm just going to have to ignore his observations and move this shit along.

"What do you need me to do about Mendez?" I ask.

Joseph squints his eyes suspiciously at me while tapping a ridiculously expensive silver Montblanc pen that Juliette bought him for his birthday a few years back on his desk.

"I paid off the three trainers, the massage therapist, and the steroids dealer, but that Doctor Edelstein is giving me problems."

"So what do you want me to do?"

"Do what you normally do. Everyone has a price so find his."

Joseph rarely asks for me to step in on jobs he's working. He's always handled his own jobs personally and only given me and the Kings the ones he didn't want to bother with. I'm not sure what his angle is today, but I don't like it.

I can't take on one more thing, not until I get my head screwed on straight.

"I'm just figuring out the clubs, Joseph, and I've got that DUI to handle—"

He cuts me off. "The Kings can handle the DUI and the clubs are just side money, Roman. Jobs like Mendez are how we all eat. You know this. That's why this needs to get done."

"How much?" I never ask Joseph details like this, but if he wants to give me more responsibility in preparation for taking over the business, it's time he stops treating me like the help. "How much is Mendez paying you for this to get done?"

"Four million up front." He says without even flinching. "And a piece of his commercial endorsements for the next three years on the backend. He just signed a five year, seventy-five million dollar contract."

"Damn."

"If even a whiff of this steroids thing gets out, he's going to lose all his endorsements, and then the government is going to start sniffing around his private life. His parents aren't documented, lived here for years, and they have no desire to start over in the Dominican Republic if they were deported. Mendez just wants to lay low and play baseball, and he's willing to pay big if we can make that happen for him. I assured him we could."

"What's the deal with the doctor?"

"I offered him half a million. He didn't budge."

"Okay … give me a week."

"A week? You can't handle it sooner?"

"No." I check the time on my cell phone.

He doesn't like my answer, but I pray that he isn't in the mood to have a full on debate about it, because I have to go right the fuck now if I'm going to make this flight.

"All right, a week."

I get up abruptly. Too abruptly.

"Got somewhere to be?"

"Just business," I say flatly.

"Business?"

"Yep." I fiddle inside my bag for another M&M and pop it in my mouth. "Need to be on time. I'll check in with you later."

"I think Juliette is cooking." He calls out as I stride down the hall. He knows Juliette's cooking is my Achilles heel. It's a test, but I'm going to have to fail this time.

"I'll grab some next time," I holler back.

He doesn't say anything else in response. He knows I'm hiding something, but he's falling back. His retreat is progress for us.

I think.

I have no idea how long Elizabeth plans on staying in the Bahamas. All I know is that she is here for a pitch meeting that the glamazon arranged, and that she is staying at The Atlantis Hotel.

It's unusual for me to fly blind like this. Usually I have Camden run a detailed search on anyone I'm trying to handle, but of course this time I'm trying to be a little more stealth-like about this shit and not tell Cam anything. Luckily Jade was able to find out the tower Elizabeth is staying in and the floor too, which is no easy task in today's world of confidentiality and privacy rights. So I guess I'm good.

I decide to handle some business during the plane ride over to keep my mind off of all the many possibilities rolling around my head about what's going on with Elizabeth and the dickweed a.k.a. Ethan.

My worst fear is that she is listening to whatever bullshit he's spouting, because I'm sure once that asshole sobered the fuck up, he realized just how much of a wreck he left in his wake, and what a good thing he fucked up. A girl like Elizabeth is definitely a good thing. The kind you wife up. Not dick around.

I decide to start my list of business phone calls to the club with the most problems. The newest one–The Lotus. Of course the manager Leroy, Larry, or whatever his name is isn't there, so I end up having to speak to the bar manager. The Rico Suave motherfucker I should have fired when I took over ownership of the club. He was sniffing all up in Elizabeth's ass the night I first saw her.

"Does Larry talk numbers with you?" I ask with little emotion.

"Yep," He responds in the same short, flat tone that I'm using.

Asshole.

"So how's the bar doing?"

"Good so far. We'll probably have a seven thousand dollar night tonight."

"We need to do more bottle service. I want a ten thousand dollar night."

"We're still–"

"I don't give a shit what we're *still* doing Mario."

I'm trying to keep my voice down since there's a suit sitting right next to me, but since I paid a lot of money for this first class seat just like he did, fuck it.

"The name's Marco."

"Whatever. Listen you're the bar manager and if you want it to stay that way, I expect you to figure out ways to raise the revenue of the bar or else what purpose do you serve? Capiche?"

"Capiche? You do know that I'm a Cuban-American right? Not an Italian mobster."

I can't believe this little shit has the nerve to be a smart-ass when he barely has a job.

"I don't fucking care," I say still trying to keep my voice low and my temper even.

"You know I saw you and her the other night right?"

"What are you talking about, Matteo?" I say in a bored to death tone, except I know exactly who and what night he's referring to.

This kid really needs to mind his fucking business and worry more about getting ballers to pop some more bottles.

"You watching her half the night, then you just happen to be there to help her out of the club when all hell breaks loose. You really should leave her alone if you haven't already messed with her head. She's a nice girl."

He picked the wrong day for this shit.

"You must not need your job do you, tough guy? You are aware that I sign your checks aren't you?"

"I've been through the last two owners, and I'll be here long after you sell the club just like they did, *Pendejo*."

I admittedly was too busy cutting class, doing dumb shit, to actually attend Senora Garcia's class in high school; but I am pretty sure Rico Suave just called me an asshole or an idiot in Spanish.

Either way I am sick of his shit. I'm sick of any and every man that feels the need to protect Elizabeth, stalk Elizabeth, hell ... look at Elizabeth. If I didn't need him to run the bar this week, I would seriously consider sending Cutter over there to break a few of his fingers just for shits and giggles.

"Just clear ten grand tough guy. I'll deal with your ass next time I see you."

"Roger that."

A text comes in before I can further cuss his smart ass out, so I hang up on him. At least I think I'm the one who hung up first.

Jade: He's definitely there.

Me: With who?

Jade: Alone.

Me: Details

Jade: Same tower as her. He was comped a suite.

Me: WTF?

Jade: I know. I'll send more details when I know.

If asshole was comped a suite, that means he's got to be gambling. He's just rolling in all sorts of addictions isn't he? I don't understand how Elizabeth hooked up with this colossal sized loser.

Now that I know he was comped a suite, I'm hoping that it is just a huge coincidence that he's there at the same time that she is. How could he know that Elizabeth was going to be there? The trip was too last minute.

But really none of that matters. Elizabeth is a sheltered suburban girl. For all I know this guy was her first love or some shit. And to make it worse, I'm worried that she may actually consider going back to him, because I scared the hell out of her when I fucked her brains out in my living room.

He better not touch her.

I swear to God he better not touch her.

I have to find her.

Then I have to fix this.

4

Elizabeth

"HEY, BITSY."

I'm sitting on an elegant leather backed stool; at the nicest hotel bar that I've probably ever been in with my eyes dramatically wide open. They are huge and unblinking. Much like the ones you see on the face of a Japanese Manga character. Ethan is the last person I expected to see in the Bahamas. No, scratch that. He's the last person I expected to see again ever.

He looks different. His clothes are well put together as usual, and he looks fit and healthy, but his eyes and the creases around his mouth tell me something different. Like he's been through something and that he's trying very hard to put up a front for me right now. A pretense that would have probably worked a couple of months ago, but one that I won't easily fall for ever again.

"You look amazing," he says way too casually to me. Like we're simply old friends catching up. As if he doesn't owe me a very detailed apology at the very least.

I stare at him dumbfounded. Struggling for the words

that would be appropriate right now. I kind of just want to slap him.

"Say something, Elizabeth."

"What do you want me to say?" I ask. Now that the initial shock is wearing off, my latent anger is beginning to step forward.

"I know you're probably pissed at me, but all I'm asking is that you hear me out."

Really?!

"You really want to do this now, Ethan? Here?"

"Actually no. I'd rather do this in my room where we can have some privacy. I have a lot to say. A lot to explain."

"Your room? Absolutely frackin' not." My voice rising higher.

He smiles uneasily.

"Ok so then where? Your room?"

The bartender places a fresh glass of sangria in front of me, quickly glances between the two of us, then walks away to take an order from another patron. Ethan places a twenty-dollar bill on the counter and takes a sip of the beer he is already holding in his hand.

"What about my drink?" I ask.

"Bring it with you to the room."

I forgot that I can easily bring my drink or anything else I decide to buy inside the hotel to my room, but that isn't really the point. I need to think straight if I am going to have a conversation with this big fat liar. I also need to ask myself why I am even entertaining the possibility of having a conversation with a guy that left me dead (for all he knew) on the floor of my apartment. What kind of man does that? Definitely not one that I ever want anything to do with again.

"I'm not sure that there is anything you can say that will change my opinion of what an ass you are, Ethan."

"I'm not trying to convince you that I'm not an ass, Bitsy. I am one. I just want to plead my case."

"Plead it for what then?"

"Your forgiveness."

I stare Ethan square in the eyes after he says the word forgiveness. I'm not an expert on human psychology or body language, so I can't say for sure whether or not he is lying to me; although my gut is telling me that he's trying too hard. I don't know if I read sincerity in his facial expressions or desperation.

I take a long swallow of my sangria, so that I can think carefully about what I'm going to say next. I'm not sure why, but suddenly Roman's face pops inside my head, and I take another sip of my drink to shake it loose.

His opinion doesn't matter, Elizabeth. This is your fight.

"I will give you ten minutes, Ethan. That's it."

I rise from my stool, smooth my skirt, and start walking. I'm embarrassed to admit this, but I make sure to walk very slowly and carefully in my heels to the elevator, one foot in front of the other, so that Ethan has a very clear view of everything he's cast aside.

When I was with Ethan, I did everything I could to camouflage the size of my hips and butt with baggy sweats or loose flowing dresses. I'd always known that while he found me attractive, he never especially cared for my figure. I didn't always feel sexy around him. But since I've been sleeping with Roman, I have to admit, that I've discovered a new found confidence and self appreciation for my shape that I've never had before.

I completely forgot that I left my room in a pretty chaotic mess while getting ready for my meeting earlier, so when we enter, I quickly start picking up clothes from the floor and begin folding them into a pile at the edge of my bed.

"Have a seat," I tell him.

"Where?" he asks sarcastically.

"Don't be a smart-ass, Ethan." I say sounding very much like a certain person I know. "Sit in the chair by the desk and start talking. Your ten minutes just started."

"Wow, you're a lot different, Bitsy."

"Getting knocked out cold by a drug dealer will do that to a girl."

I notice Ethan's slight flinch at my comment. Good, at least he is showing some sign of remorse or at least guilt because for the last few weeks, I've seriously considered that Ethan must be some sort of sociopath in order to not give a shit about the havoc he's brought into my life.

I stop gathering and folding clothes when Ethan grabs me gently by the wrist.

"I have a drug problem, Elizabeth," he says with earnest. "I hid it from you, from my teammates, from everyone."

If he's looking for sympathy, I'm not ready to give it to him.

"Who were those men that broke into my apartment, and hurt me, and stole my money, Ethan?"

"What money?" He asks incredulously.

I can't tell if he's lying, and it's annoying that I have to second-guess everything he says.

"Why are you acting clueless all of a sudden, Ethan? All the money I saved working at The Tavern. The money I told you I was going to live on for the next year. It was hidden in some empty tampon boxes in my bathroom."

"I knew you were saving, Bitsy, but you never said that it was in the house. I didn't know they took your money. I didn't know that there was any money to take."

Not likely. I'm sure I'd mentioned at least once that I had money stashed in my apartment.

"So what do you know about that night exactly?" I ask.

"They were men that I bought drugs from and as I got further up shit's creek, they turned into men I sold drugs for. I owed them a shitload of money, and I couldn't ask my parents for it. They'd obviously know something was up. So I thought I'd sell temporarily to make the money back. Kids were buying drugs anyway on campus, so I figured why not from me?

"But I didn't realize just how hard it is to deal on campus, and I wasn't moving it fast enough. I was late on my payments, and I thought I had a little more time to figure things out, but they decided the night we were together that I was out of time. They had been following us the whole night."

Okay, so that explains why he was acting weird that whole night. His sixth sense must have been trying to tell him something. That and the fact that he was probably high.

"So why did you act like you didn't know what they were talking about when they asked you about the drugs? When they threatened to hurt me if you didn't answer correctly. You made them angry, Ethan. Purposely. Why would you let them hurt me knowing that you had their drugs the whole time?"

I'm doing my best not to break down in tears for the millionth time over this whole thing. Just reliving that whole night makes me very emotional though. Not just because it was painful to be hit by a grown man (because it was), but more so because I'd been betrayed by someone I trusted. Someone I had just moments ago given my body to. Someone I thought could possibly be my forever guy.

"Because I was high that night. Because I was in over my head. Because—"

"You're a natural born liar."

"That's right, Bitsy," he sighs. "Because I'm a liar and a coward."

"So you were definitely high then when we had sex?"

"Yes." Ethan hangs his head low with his response.

I'm not sure I should have even asked him that. The knowledge of it makes me feel empty. It was all meaningless for him.

"I did my best to keep it away from you, Bitsy, but sometimes I just couldn't help myself. I talked myself into believing that I had things under control when it's obvious now that I didn't. I was high during many important moments over the last two years, but I most regret being high on that night. Especially because I was with you."

He's saying all the right things, but I'm not totally sold. I check the neon green numbers on the alarm clock to see how long he's been talking. I want to make sure that I stick to my ten minute rule. If I let him talk too long, I may falter and actually forgive his lying butt.

"And why did I wake up alone after being knocked out? Where did you go?"

"They made me take them to where I had the rest of the drugs stashed. They wanted them back, and they weren't taking no for an answer. I couldn't call an ambulance for you. I couldn't do shit. I actually thought it was the best thing I could do for you. Getting them the hell out of there I mean."

Oh please.

"And why aren't you still in a rehab in Arizona like your rude ass father told me you were? If you have such a drug problem, shouldn't you be there?"

"I know my dad's an ass. I'm sorry for whatever he may have said to you."

"He tried to pay me off, Ethan. Pay me to not say anything about what happened that night. Pay me to not take your calls. Although you never called, so that wasn't really an issue was it?"

Ethan hangs his head down even lower.

"I'm sorry. I didn't know he did that."

"He didn't even ask how I was. He doesn't think too much of me I take it. Just like his son."

Silence.

"So continue," I say. "What happened with rehab?"

"I left rehab."

"Really? Why did you do that? Because you haven't been in there long enough to go through any sort of real treatment program."

"I signed myself out. Truth is I have to find a swim club that will take me in, so I can get my life back on track, before I blow my chance, Bitsy. I can't do that in a residential treatment facility. Swimming is my future. The Olympics is all I've ever wanted. It's all I've got. I can find an out treatment program at home."

"Home?"

"In Philly."

"You're coming back to Philadelphia?"

I'm absolutely appalled that he'd move back. The city is not big enough for the two of us. It just isn't.

"Yes, for a lot of reasons."

He looks at me pitifully as if to insinuate that I'm one of those reasons.

Oh hell to the no!

"Well your ten minutes are up, and I think I've heard everything that I need to hear. Oh wait a minute, not everything. I just want to know what you're doing here in The Bahamas?"

"Just getting a little rest before I get back to the real world."

"So this is a vacation for you?" I ask incredulously.

"I guess you could call it that."

He looks at me as if he's hesitant to say more. As if he feels guilty for enjoying his life. Good. He should feel like crap.

"Unbelievable."

"What is?"

"That you happen to coincidentally see me at a bar in the frackin' Bahamas. I mean what are the chances."

"Maybe it's fate."

"I doubt it." I roll my eyes. "One more question, Ethan. When were you planning on contacting me to apologize? To check and see if I was even alive and well? It's been weeks and you're out here frackin' vacationing? I didn't deserve one phone call?"

"I swear I was coming straight to you when I got back to Philly, Bitsy. You were going to be my first stop. I wanted to get my shit together first. I didn't want to come to you a mess."

"I don't live in that apartment anymore. You wouldn't have found me."

"We have plenty of mutual friends. Just because you moved doesn't mean I wouldn't have found you."

"Our mutual friends seem to only be your friends now. I haven't spoken to any of them since this whole thing happened."

"No one?" he asks suspiciously.

"What are you insinuating?"

"Haven't you been talking to Jagger?"

"How do you know that?"

Has Jagger been telling him?

"Like I said, we have mutual friends that make it their business to keep me updated on you. You're my girl, Bitsy. No matter how much I messed up, you are still my sweet, smart girlfriend who I'm going to marry one day. I just need to prove to you that I'm okay now."

I'm still standing in the middle of the room, shifting side to side uncomfortably. I'm listening to the words coming out of his mouth, and immediately all I can think about is Roman. I'm thinking that even if I considered for one moment taking Ethan back, what that would mean for the two of us.

"So where are you living now, and why are you in the Bahamas?" He asks.

"You don't have the privilege of asking me questions about my life Ethan."

Ethan stands up and moves closer to me.

"You've really changed, Bitsy."

And for the first time since I've known Ethan … I feel absolutely nothing.

"Yeah, you keep saying that."

5

Elizabeth

THERE IS A SUDDEN, urgent, knocking at the door of my hotel room. Whoever it is doesn't have the common decency to knock like a normal person, but instead pounds on my door like they're the frackin' police. With my drug dealing ex in my room, goodness knows it just may just be the police.

Ethan moves quickly to answer the door before I have a chance to. Like he's worried that it may be trouble coming again for him. Or perhaps he considers his charge to the door as an act of protection of me, since he did such a piss poor job of it not so long ago. Seeing him walk with some sort of valiant purpose to answer my door reminds me for just a moment some of what I used to see in him. At least physically.

Ethan has a tall, lean swimmer's body and the face of a celebrity, which I found very attractive once upon a time. And while he's not drop dead yummy like Roman (although I hate to even make the comparison); Ethan has always had an air of confidence about him that I didn't see in most twenty or twenty-one year old guys at school. Of course all of that was attractive, until it wasn't any longer. Until I learned the hard way that it was all a huge lie. A front.

He attempts looking through the peephole to see who it is on the other side of the door, but the peephole appears to be purposely covered.

"Who is it?" Ethan asks through the door in an octave lower than his normal voice.

It would be almost comical if I wasn't worried about who was on the other side my damn self.

The pounding stops and now there is an eerie silence.

I feel a tingle across the back of my neck, and then I immediately recognize the voice spewing angry words that are being said loud enough for the entire floor of the hotel to hear.

"Open this fucking door right now cocksucker."

My heart begins thumping so loudly, that I'm afraid it will pump straight through my chest. For a fleeting moment, I think I see fear shoot across Ethan's face, and then next I notice confusion. He's not sure who this is on the other side of my door, but also seems relieved that he doesn't recognize the voice.

But of course I do.

"Who are you calling a cocksucker asshole?" Ethan whips the door open with a false sense of bravado.

I feel a bit of déjà vu, because once again I'm sitting on the edge of my bed, frightened as hell at the possibility of what may happen next. Just like the night of the attack. Except this time is slightly different. This time there isn't some dead-eyed, Shrek-covered, criminal itching to hurt me. This time it's my wild-eyed cousin itching to beat the shit out of at least one of us.

He is fuming.

The scar under his left eye twitching.

His fingers curling and flexing.

And he's so frackin' beautiful right now that it hurts. Damn I missed him, and it hasn't even been that long.

"Is there any other cocksucker in this room?" Roman asks in a very antagonistic fashion, as he pushes his way through the threshold and allows the door to slam shut.

He's staring daggers at me and holds my eyes in a lock that seems to be accusatory. I don't know if I should blink first, look away, or start talking. So I try not to do any one of those three things. It may be in everyone's best interest if I don't, until I know for sure where Roman's head is at.

"What the fuck," Roman says to me in a bone chilling voice.

"What are you doing here?" I ask. Knowing immediately after I say it that it was the wrong question to ask.

"Elizabeth," he says with a strong note of warning.

"This is Ethan," I tell him quietly.

"I know who the fuck it is," Roman growls. "The question is what the fuck is he doing inside of your room?"

Ethan quickly snaps his head between us both in confusion.

"Is THIS who you're fucking now, Bitsy?" Ethan points in Roman's direction. "THIS is what you've lowered–"

Ethan isn't able to finish the rest of his sentence, because in a matter of seconds Roman clutches his throat with one hand and won't let go. He's gripping him with the power of the jaws of a pit bull but seems to be doing it with little effort.

Like it's easy.

And with a sneer on his face as if he enjoys it.

I can't watch anymore as Ethan gasps for air, so I jump off the bed to put an end to it before he either passes out or someone hears the scuffle and calls hotel security.

"Roman stop," I plead.

"I asked you why the fuck he is in here."

He turns his head towards me with purpose while still calmly choking the ever-living shit out of my jerk of an ex-boyfriend. I gently touch his forearm to hopefully get his attention and to stop him from catching a murder charge.

"Roman," I say softly. "If you don't let him go, then he can't go anywhere, and he was definitely about to leave."

Roman tilts his head to the side and watches me for a moment, analyzing me as he often does with his internal bullshit meter; then he turns his attention back to Ethan.

"Listen to me closely … Ethan. Whatever shit you're up to ends now. You were responsible for some filthy ass dealer putting his hands on Elizabeth. Just for that alone, I should squeeze your throat until you bust a blood vessel, but that's not what this is about. It's not about what I want. It's about what she wants, and what my cousin wants is you gone and out of her life. Do we understand each other?"

Ethan is turning a frightening shade of purple. And is it crazy for me to think right at this moment that I wish Roman wasn't so quick to announce to the whole world that we're cousins? Maybe I wanted Ethan to think for just a moment that I have moved on with the bad-ass literally holding his next breath in his hands.

"Roman," I say again while this time touching his back. "I don't think he can answer you."

"Fuck," he mutters as if he doesn't realize his own strength.

When Roman releases Ethan's throat, I watch his Adam's apple finally move again and then he takes a couple gulps of air. I actually feel a little sorry for him, but not as much as I probably should.

"You're her cousin?" Ethan asks through strained breaths.

"That's right, and I promise you that if you even

breathe in her direction again, that I will put you down like the dog that you are."

For the first time since Ethan walked into my hotel room, I finally see what I think is an honest emotion cross his face … trepidation.

"Roman, I'm going to go out in the hall and speak with Ethan for a moment. I need you to stay in here okay?"

He looks at me like I have lost my last little bit of sense.

"Elizabeth," he exhales harshly. "Fuck no."

"Just five minutes?" I beg.

He rubs his hands back and forth across the top of his head out of frustration.

"Two minutes," he barks.

"I need five."

"I don't like this shit."

I can see that Roman is struggling with some sort of internal battle. He's not used to compromise. He's not used to the art of negotiation, at least not without the use of his fists. He's used to setting the terms and fuck anyone who doesn't agree.

"I didn't know Bitsy had a cousin," Ethan chimes in.

Why is he speaking? I guess he isn't as threatened by Roman, now that he thinks that he's only my cousin and not someone I'm sleeping with (of course that in it of itself is hysterical).

"I won't hurt her man," he continues. "I just want to talk to her."

"I know you won't hurt her prick."

Roman grins almost like a psychotic killer.

"Ethan don't say anything else," I plead.

I pull Roman to the side. His breath heavy and his eyes practically dilated and fixed on Ethan the entire time.

"Roman," I grab his face with both of my hands and

turn his head to face mine. "Let me have my final five minutes with him. I just need closure."

After what seems like forever, his face starts to soften. Then he starts rubbing a few strands of my hair between his thumb and pointer finger. I'm sure Ethan thinks I'm related to some sort of psychopath with questionable boundary issues at this point.

"Why do you want to talk to him?" he asks quietly. I can tell he's calming down. Starting to see reason.

"I don't expect you to understand. It's total girl shit. It's just that whatever Ethan and I went through, he did once mean something to me. This needs to at least end with a five minute conversation between us."

"Didn't this ass-wipe have his five minutes when you were sprawled across the floor of your apartment unconscious and he left. Isn't that all the fucking closure you need?"

I sigh in exasperation. Roman isn't making this easy, and I hate that we're hashing this out completely in front of Ethan.

"Roman–"

"Didn't you say your money was stolen that night?"

I don't know why he's bringing this up now or where he's going with it.

"Yes."

Ethan continues to stand silently but attentively watching the exchange between us.

"How much?"

I keep my lips clamped together. Roman's never asked me how much money was taken before. I've never told a soul how much was in there, not even Sloan, because it's embarrassing. I can hear all of the I told you so's already. Only paranoid old folks hide large sums of money in their houses. Not twenty somethings from the burbs.

"That's not important because—"

"Second time I'm asking, Elizabeth. How fucking much?"

Crap.

"Seventeen."

"Seventeen what, hundred?"

"Thousand," I whisper. Wishing that he wasn't forcing this issue. Geez, Roman has no sense of boundaries or privacy.

Ethan's eyes bulge at my revelation. At least I know now that he didn't really know about the money or at least how much was there.

"So let me get this straight," Roman says practically gritting his teeth. "You need additional closure with a man who brought scum to your home, scum that stole seventeen fucking thousand dollars from you, scum who knocked you the fuck out and who is responsible for you having to move out of your own apartment?"

"Roman, I—"

"And what has he been saying to you while he's been in here? Bitsy, I'm so sorry." He says imitating a whiny voice. "Bitsy, I messed up. Fuck that! Your druggie-ass, superstar swimmer is just sorry that he got exposed. I bet he's been saying some slick shit out of his mouth to try and get you back hasn't he? Did he tell you that he hasn't been in Arizona at all? That he hasn't been in rehab ever?"

"What?" I turn to look at Ethan. Is he still playing me?

"Wait one damn minute—" Ethan interrupts.

"No you wait a minute," I say angrily as Roman takes a step in front of me, and closer to Ethan. Just a few mere inches away from his face. Completely towering over him.

"Don't say anything else cocksucker, or I swear I will beat you down just for the hell of it."

"You don't scare "

Crack!

Roman hits Ethan with a single overhead punch dropping him straight to the carpeted floor; I silently cover my mouth with my hands in shock.

"Since you seem to be the chatty type," Roman speaks at Ethan while he's sprawled out on the floor. "I'll go ahead and give you three minutes to talk to Elizabeth outside of this room where I don't have to lay eyes on your ugly ass again, but let me be clear, it will be the last three minutes you will have with her for the rest of your life. After that, forget that she's in this hotel. Forget she exists."

Ethan stands up on wobbly legs and wipes a small drop of blood oozing from the corner of his mouth. He stares coldly at Roman for what seems like the longest sixty seconds of my life, and then he smirks and moves toward the door and opens it.

"After you, Bitsy," he says to me in an extra flirty way.

He's got balls. I'll give Ethan that.

"Don't fucking call her that!" Roman roars.

I see a recognizable glint of satisfaction sparkling in Ethan's eyes. He thoroughly enjoyed that he was able to at least instigate that outburst from Roman.

"I don't like your cousin," Ethan says to me out in the hallway.

"That's all right," I say annoyed. "He doesn't like you either."

"He's weird with you."

"Yeah?" I say like I don't have any idea what he's talking about, especially because I don't think I really give two cents what he thinks.

"He treats you like a possession. Like you're his property."

Sometimes I think I am. Or that I desperately want to be.

"He's just intense," I wave my hand to change the conversation. "Listen … I just wanted to tell you that I'm trying really hard to put everything that happened with you behind me. I didn't bring the police into it for a reason. I just want to move on with my life.

"I'm trying to build a new business and live quietly. I don't care that you lied about rehab, I don't really give a rats ass where you've been, although I don't understand why you felt the need to lie to me. I just want to make it crystal clear that when you move back to Philly, I think it's best that you don't contact me at all."

"Tick. Tock." Roman's verbal warning comes crisp and clear through the door.

"Bitsy, we were good together for a year. I waited for you for a year. Everything was fine between us until that night. I want a second chance. There are worse people like murderers and rapists who get second chances. I was sick. An addict. I'm getting better now on my own, and all I'm asking for is a second chance. If you give me a second, I can explain everything about rehab. Your cousin doesn't have it right. Just give me a chance to explain."

"It doesn't really matter anymore, Ethan. I'm sorry but no."

I don't even think that I'm really sorry at all, but it sounds like the right thing to say. Actually turning him down feels like the best thing I've done in a long time. Looking back, I realize we were never right for each other anyway. Drugs or no drugs.

"This isn't done. We aren't done, Bitsy."

The hotel room door opens.

"Three minutes is up, motherfucker. You're very much

done. Come inside now, Elizabeth." Roman says while looking straight into the eyes of Ethan with deadly calm.

I give one last glance to the man I thought would possibly be my future and say goodbye. A final goodbye.

"Bye, Ethan."

I don't know why, but I feel a little melancholy about it. Like a chapter of my life has been written to completion. A necessary close to that chapter, but it doesn't make it any less sad.

"Not bye, Bitsy, just later," Ethan says as he walks down the hall towards the elevator.

"Whatever, motherfucker," Roman says to Ethan's back.

But I know that Ethan's just saving face. We're done and he knows it. I mean he must know it. How could I ever trust him again after all that's happened? All the lies he's told. He's got to know that. He's not a complete idiot, and if I want to be brutally honest with myself right now, he was never that into me anyway. He was always distracted with swimming, with other girls, and evidently also with getting high.

"I better not see one fucking tear roll down your face," Roman snarls at me as I move past him to go back inside the room.

"Oh shut up, Roman."

6

Roman

"ARE YOU AWAKE?"

"What time is it?" I ask with a scratchy rasp and sleep in my voice.

"I don't know. Probably check out time."

After I stood in the hallway and watched Mr. Ethan Dumbfuck get on the elevator and out of my cousin's life for good, Elizabeth and I both returned inside the room and got totally twisted on mini bar alcohol for the rest of the night.

I mixed us my own version of Bahamian Rum punch, ordered us two plates of conch and pigeon peas from room service, and then we actually made it through two and a half movies (her choice) before we passed out.

In the middle of all of that, I cussed her the hell out for leaving the country without telling me, and she admonished me for flying all the way here without permission. As if I give a fuck about getting permission.

After we got all of that out of the way, I asked her how she thought her pitch meeting went, and then she spent the next twenty minutes reenacting her entire pitch with a little commentary on the side.

I assured her that it sounded great to me and that her tight ass pencil skirt probably went a long way in sealing the deal (she put the skirt back on as part of the reenactment scene for effect). She looked sexy as fuck. I think I must have laughed all night. Outwardly a couple of times and inside my head many, many more times. That's just how easy things can be between us.

I also made sure that I didn't touch her. And that was no easy feat seeing as how we've just slept in the same bed. I promised myself that if it was going to ever happen again between us, she was going to have to ask for it. Preferably beg for it. I'm not going to be responsible for scaring the hell out of her a second time by moving too fast. Although I've been known to bend my own rules from time to time.

"What time is your flight?" I ask her with ulterior motives.

My dick is brick hard and aching.

I make sure to keep the pristine Egyptian cotton sheets covering my morning wood as I roll my body over closer to hers. We're on our sides, her back against my chest, with only the sheet between my boxers and her vintage Rolling Stones T-shirt and red panties.

Dammit.

I can feel my will bending and breaking. I'm not sure I can wait for her to ask for it. I take a long eye-fucking look of her lush body and can't but help but start to run the backs of my fingertips along the curves of her body. I start at the crease of her armpit and travel along the side of her breast, the dip of her waist, the arc of her hips, and finally down to her smooth thighs. I can only imagine what they'd both feel like draped over my shoulders as I stroked deep and long inside of her.

Like absolute fucking heaven.

"What are you doing?" She asks with a flirty tone that I'm all too familiar with. It's the voice universally used by women everywhere. I know what it means. It's a green light to take this wherever I want to take it.

But didn't I just say I wanted her to beg?

Damn, I'm a weak fucker.

"Nothing quite yet, but why don't you just tell me what it is you want me to do to you."

There's silence between us for a moment. A bit of heavy breathing. She's making the decision right now. I feel a slight bit of tension in her body, but that doesn't mean she's going to shut this down. In my experience, it could mean that she's simply getting the nerve up to tell me exactly what she really wants. I hope like hell it's the latter.

"I want you to touch me."

Motherfucking bingo.

"Touch you where?" I ask provocatively.

"Under my shirt."

"Under your shirt where?" I ask while softly licking the rim of her ear.

She lets out a few little soft gasps and then a few giggles.

"Here." she touches her breasts. "And also down there. Inside my panties."

I love this sexy, playful side of her.

"You do, huh?"

"I really do."

We're both laying on our right sides, so I reach my left arm around and slide it down inside the front of her panties.

"Goddammit you're soaking, Duchess."

"I know," she whispers.

"How did you get yourself in such a state?" I tease.

"From thinking about you all night."

My grin is a mile wide, but I keep it to myself, since I'm still lying behind her.

"Thinking about what, baby?"

"Your face in between my legs."

That may not be her begging, but it's a strong ass fucking request. So I decide to comply by unwrapping the sheet from around me and sliding my head down under it and in between her legs. And I can't wait because I love the taste and smell of Elizabeth's pussy.

I think it's my new addiction.

I'm not going to lie and say that it smells like strawberries or fresh rain showers; any man who says that is a fucking liar. But what I will say is that she has a taste and scent that is completely unique to her, one that lets me know that she's very happy to see me. A mixture of salt, musk, want, need and pleasure that is totally distinctive to her, and one that I crave like a fat kid loves cake.

While I'm happy as fuck to be in between my cousin's legs, I can't forget the details of what brought me here. Why I'm blowing off work. Why I just overpaid for a typically affordable airplane ticket. Why I can't seem to get my head on straight when it comes to her.

Well maybe I can forget why for just a little bit longer.

"How do you know how to do that?" she asks in complete rapture. "You're ruining me."

"That's the objective, baby."

"Oh. My. God!"

I can feel her body tensing as the slow winding orgasm builds higher inside of her. She's ready to come for me, but she's been a naughty girl, and I can't let that shit slide. That's why I immediately stop all licking, sucking and kissing.

"Roman," she cries out in frustration. Beating her fist against the mattress.

"I don't want you to ever take a trip like this again without calling me first, Elizabeth."

"I told Joseph and Juliette where I was going," she protests.

"I don't have shit to do with that. You and I both know that this is way past Joseph asking me to keep an eye on you. We have our own relationship now, which is separate and apart from Joseph and Juliette. Wouldn't you agree?"

"I guess so."

"What now?"

"Yes, Roman. Yes."

"Good. I'm glad you're starting to see the light. Now you knew I was probably going crazy at home when I found out you were in the Bahamas all alone right?"

"Well not exactly. I'm a grown ass woman. Why would you be sick with worry? It makes zero sense."

"Zero sense when your cell phone wasn't working, and your sorry ass ex is here stalking you?"

"He isn't stalking me," she says rubbing her legs together like a horny cricket.

If I wasn't trying to prove a point right now, I'd kiss the hell out of her. She wants me inside her so badly, and I'm the lucky son of a bitch who is going to get to come inside. Pun absolutely intended.

"Please, can we stop talking about him?" she asks.

I laugh to myself.

"We sure can baby, but let me just finish my thought. Your sudden disappearing act was a distraction for me, and I don't like distractions. My business is very important to me."

"So what are you saying?"

"I'm saying spread your fucking legs and take your punishment like a good girl."

She smiles as if she won some sort of prize. Totally misunderstanding what I'm about to do to her.

She'll understand soon.

"Ok," she agrees softly.

I smile and then return back to what is turning out to be my new favorite place on earth.

Between my cousin's legs.

Elizabeth

A THIN LAYER OF sweat covers my trembling body as I clench the sheets of the California king bed that I'm spread eagle on. I have had three earth shattering orgasms in the last fifteen minutes thanks to the extraordinary skills of one Mr. Roman Masterson, and while I appreciate the effort, I don't think that I'm physically capable of having another.

I'm pretty sure if I do that my head may explode. If I could, I would run out of this room and jump into the hotel lagoon to cool off and come down off of this orgasm high. But that seems to be Mr. Masterson's sinister plan or punishment, because he's only stopping for a moment in between orgasms, to talk to me, and give me a second to come down, and then he starts it all over again.

And again.

And again.

"You're so fucking beautiful." He says while methodically stroking the inside of my thighs with his thumbs, the rest of his hands kneading my hips. The sensation of his callused hands rubbing against my dewy skin purposely keeping me slightly simmering but not quite blazing hot for him.

"Roman," I moan.

"Yes, baby."

"I need you to stop."

"I'm not stopping."

"Do you really want my parents to bear the shame of burying a daughter who died at the hands of an orgasm?"

"You mean multiple orgasms."

"Yes, you sadist. Multiple orgasms."

"A sadist would enjoy hurting you. That's not what I do. This doesn't hurt does it, Duchess?"

"Stop calling me that."

"Now why would I do that?"

"'Cause I'm mad at you."

He starts sliding one of his thick fingers inside of my sex, then back out, and then in again. It's the second entry that makes me arch my back off the bed. When he pulls his finger back out the second time he slides it slowly inside his mouth and sucks hard.

"Mmmm."

"You're so frackin' nasty." I say pretending not to be totally turned on by what he just did.

"And you're so fucking wet for me." He chuckles. "Can you even say the word fucking, Duchess?"

I shake my head no. "I don't say that or the p word. Well I say the p word to myself but never out loud."

"You mean the word pussy?"

And before I can respond, Roman's mouth is covering my mouth. I can taste a hint of myself on his tongue as he thrusts it expertly inside. He kisses the same way he does everything. Setting the tempo, doing it as if he was born already knowing what to do, and enjoying every minute of it.

One of his hands makes it way back between my legs and he starts fingering me again while using his thumb to rub back and forth over my clit. I'm utterly exhausted, but it's like my body has a mind of its own and responds willingly to every one of Roman's ministrations.

"Masterson—" I sigh.

"I love it when you call my name out baby, but this time I'm going to need you to say it louder. Loud enough that everyone on this floor knows whose pussy this belongs to."

I wish he'd stop frackin' talking!

I'm trying my best to hold off this next orgasm. I'm trying everything to get my head out of the game. I think of oral book reports, global warming, and those god-awful animal cruelty commercials, but none of it's working.

Everything he says makes me hornier, and everything he's doing feels ridiculously good especially the loud smack he gives me on my right ass cheek.

"Open your eyes now."

"You didn't have to smack my butt," I falsely protest.

"I think I did have to, and I think you liked it. You're even wetter now, and I've got your full attention."

Roman starts working a second hard-edged finger inside of my core and moving his thumb more rapidly across my clit. It's taking a lot longer for my orgasm to build this time and it's blissfully excruciating. Each one is taking longer than the last, but it's coming. It started as a dull ache that is building into a crescendo of pure agony.

"You ever been fucked, Duchess?"

Is he kidding right now? He can't possibly think I'm going to have an X-rated Q&A session while he's doing all of this to me.

"I can do this shit all night." He grins devilishly. "You'd do best to answer me."

"Obviously, Roman. You know better than anyone that I'm not a virgin."

His hand stops. "No baby. I mean fucked well and properly."

"If the sex I had with you before counts ... then yes."

He chuckles. "I can do better than that."

He slides back under the covers where his head disappears, and in exactly one more minute I come so hard that my eyes roll into the back of my head, and my hands and feet start to tingle.

"Oh God! "

"Who?" He bites gently on my clit; further drawing out my climax.

"Masterson!"

"That's fucking right baby. Next time say the right name the first time. God has nothing to do with this."

"Next time?" I cry.

"Oh fuck yeah. I figure you have about three or four more left in you even if it takes us all day to get you there. This is your punishment, Elizabeth."

"I've got to check out of the room. I don't have all day to subject myself to your brand of torture."

"I'll take care of it."

"I don't want you in between my legs all day." Did I really just say that?

"You're an awful liar, Duchess. You know you want me right here," he gently pats my pussy. "All fucking day."

"I'm not lying. You're just incredibly arrogant."

Roman gave me a fifteen minute break in between orgasms, so that he could call down to the front desk and book my room an additional night, even though he already has his own room on the same floor. Something about not giving me the chance to put on any clothes. This way I'd stay "naked and spread" all day for him is how I think the Neanderthal put it.

I am starting to feel dirty. Well … dirtier. Almost like I'm his personal sex slave, except for the obvious fact that I am reaping all the benefits of this arrangement.

I'm at orgasm seven.

My clitoris is swollen and over-sensitized. My head is pounding from the constant adrenaline rush to my brain. Tears are starting to fall. I literally can't take anymore. This is definitely an exquisite punishment, but I think it needs to stop before I pass the hell out. I'm not sure he cares though; he's enjoying every minute of this, maybe more than I am. If that's even possible.

"Roman," I say seriously.

"Elizabeth," he retorts.

"You've made your point."

"Have I?"

"I was a bad girl. I didn't call you before I left."

"And?"

"And I allowed Ethan up to my room when I should have ignored him entirely."

"And?"

I thought hard.

"And … I don't know."

"The money."

"Oh and I didn't tell you how much money they took from me?"

He smiles in approval. "Exactly. And of course there's the bigger issue."

"Bigger than all of that?"

"I think I moved things too fast in my apartment the other night. Wouldn't you agree?"

"Doesn't seem to be any different than what is happening right here in this hotel room. Wouldn't you agree?" I retort sarcastically.

"I know and that's the bigger issue. I can't keep my hands off of you. I want to fuck you in the worst way. All the time. Everyday."

I'm speechless, and it damn sure isn't because of his flattering albeit crude words, but because I'm starting to feel the same exact way, and he and I both know this won't work. That this has nowhere to go but to the intersection of end and badly.

"I'm not sure what to say to that flowery declaration of whatever the frack." I say with a sarcastic twang.

Roman's laugh lightens the heaviness in the room.

"I demand you say the word fuck right now."

"No."

He starts to tickle me under my armpits.

"Say it."

"No," I manage to say through a snort.

"Say it."

"Aaaah! Stop tickling me jerk off. I can't breathe," I beg.

"Say it and I'll stop."

"All right already! FUCK!"

He finally stops.

"Now was that so bad, nerd?"

That's when I whack Roman upside his head with a pillow and the longest pillow fight of my life ensues. I'm sick of him calling me a nerd, I've heard it all my life, so I try my best to hit him as hard as I can.

Usually a good thump on top of the head works (well it did when I was ten years old), but he's much taller than me, even with me standing and him sitting on his knees on the bed. So he's getting the best of me and knocking me back on my ass with every wallop.

"Oh my God, stop hitting me so hard." I laugh hysterically as I try ducking from the next blow.

"It's either this ass whipping I'm giving you or your next orgasm. I know you've been counting them. What number am I on?"

Whack!

"My ears are ringing you, Neanderthal. Stop it."

"Ass whipping or orgasm? You pick."

Thump!

At last I get one good shot in even though he doesn't even flinch. That's when he grabs me by both of my upper arms and stares me forcefully in the eyes.

"Orgasm it is."

Just the gravelly roughness of his voice instantly sends a gush of moisture between my legs, and I realize that no matter how much I pretend that I don't want it I'd rather have death by orgasm at the hands of this man any frackin' day.

Roman quickly tosses me down on the bed, straddles my hips, then lifts my arms up over my head. I'm hesitant to keep them there, because he just spent the last few minutes tickling me to death under my pits, but I hold them still.

"Keep your hands up there. Don't move them. I'm going to try something."

"What?"

He ignores me and gets up to grab a few melting ice cubes from the ice bucket and tosses them in his mouth. Then he moves slowly towards my right breast and circles my nipple with his now frigid tongue. My nipple pebbles almost immediately, and I inadvertently groan in approval.

I start to spread my legs a little wider as a subtle invitation for him to keep up the good work, but he isn't falling for my trickery. The sadist that he is wants to draw this whole episode out.

"Uh-uh, Duchess. Keep those legs clamped shut."

He continues the magical shit he is doing with his tongue and teeth by adding a few more cubes to his mouth and moving to my left nipple. The sensitive one.

I can tell by his handling of this breast that he is fully aware that I am more sensitive on this side than the other. He isn't as rough with this nipple. He's slower and more precise about how he flicks his tongue back and forth, and then around and around, ending each pattern with a tiny kiss on the underside of my breast.

He decides to do one of his famous spot checks and slides his middle finger along the slit of my sex and is pleased with what he finds.

"Perfect wet pussy."

The words are enough to send me to the precipice, but I'm not quite ready to topple over just yet. Roman continues teasing, suckling, and savoring my breasts over and over with an occasional spot check down below, and as if he has some sort of sixth sense and knows I'm about to blow, he gives my pussy a quick hard slap and that's when I fall completely off the cliff and into a blissful, orgasmic state of hell yes!

"That was number eight," I pant and say with a smile.

"My lucky number. I think I'll stop it there."

I rub my legs together, because unbelievably I don't want him to stop. I need more of him."

"Oh, but does my Duchess want something more?"

He knows that I do.

"Does she?" he asks again.

"Yes."

"What do you want? Tell me." He grins.

"I want—"

I can't say the words. I've only had sex with Roman once, and one time is a mistake, but twice is ridiculous. I know that everything we've been doing today is no frackin' better, but at least I can say with a straight face that we haven't exactly been fucking like bunnies. At least I can say it was a one-time thing. If I have sex with him again, right now, I won't be able to even say that.

"I want … I want to go home, Roman."

Roman pauses for a moment and stares at me as if he's looking straight through my eyes and into the back of my head. I'm pretty sure he's pissed, and that's putting it mildly.

He stands up, pulls the jeans he had on yesterday back on and simply orders me to, "Get dressed."

"Where are you going?" I asked slightly panicked that I've completely ruined one of the best days of my life.

"To get showered, get my shit, and get us both the hell out of here and back to the real world."

As soon as I hear the door click shut with him on the other side a few tears begin to fall.

8

Elizabeth

ROMAN DID SOME juggling and was able to book a business class seat on my same flight back to Philly. Our seats aren't next to each other though, and I am a little surprised that he hasn't bothered to ask his neighbor or mine if either of them would consider switching seats. Although it appears that the brunette practically salivating in the seat next to him would put up a fight if anyone dared to ask her to switch. I don't dare ask myself, since I am assuming that this is another one of his punishments or more accurately put, this is Roman pouting.

I don't understand how a man that does whatever the heck he does everyday to make a massive living can act so much like a little baby. I guess this is what my mother was talking about when she said that men are all just little boys inside nice, muscular packaging. This describes Roman to a T.

In my last ditch effort to make a final impression and thank Mr. Lambert for his extraordinary hospitality, I left him a hand written note at the front desk. I'm thinking about all the millions of ways I wish I could have rewritten that letter, when the pilot announces that we can finally use our electronic equipment and the plane's WiFi, now that the aircraft is cruising at a steady altitude.

Since I have over three hours to kill, and no Roman to talk to, I decide to write Sloan a letter. Her email goes straight to her cell phone, so I know that she'll get it right away.

Hey,

I'm headed back to Philly right now. By the time you get home from work I should have pooped (you know I don't poop well when I travel), showered, and changed and we can head out for a cocktail or two:).

The pitch meeting went as well as I think it could have gone. I was prepared and while they had some tough questions for me, all of them were valid. I'm not sure my business is an appealing enough opportunity for men that invest millions of dollars everyday in way more important stuff—but if anything, it was a great opportunity and a great learning experience. So thanks for setting it up.

Your guy was kind of hot by the way:) I forgot how good-looking he was. What ever happened with him anyway? Oh yeah, he had some obsession with meeting your dad right?

Speaking of guys, you're not going to like this, in fact you're probably going to rip my head off, but there's something I've been keeping from you and I don't think I can do it any longer. I've been messing around with Roman. Yes, that's right—my cousin Roman. And it's bad. We'll talk more about it later I'm sure:)

-Bitsy

I can feel him glaring at me.

In fact I can always feel Roman from the floor to the ceiling whenever he's in the vicinity. It's understandably more obvious now, because he's only sitting a few feet away from me, but proximity doesn't particularly matter. Not when it comes to us. When he's anywhere nearby, it's as if my brain recognizes his energy in the room and sends my body physical signals to react.

Signals to acknowledge his presence.

Like my skin prickling.

Panties moist.

I reluctantly turn my head as if I actually have a choice in the matter and notice the scowl on his beautifully scarred face. He stares me down as if he's daring me to look away first.

Once again he's angry with me for being the only grown up in the room. He and I both know that this thing between us can't end well. That we aren't stars in the middle of some damn romantic comedy where all ends well with a jaw dropping kiss while an old '80s power ballad plays in the background.

That's why I make the decision to turn away first. Like I said, someone has to be the responsible adult here and stop this before it gets totally out of hand.

I look back down at my inbox to check all my unread emails (mostly junk) that I didn't check while sunning all day (and playing with Roman all night); I notice there's one from Jagger.

Hi Elizabeth,

I saw Sloan at Java today and she told me you were away on business. Didn't want to disturb you, so I thought I'd email you instead of texting. I'm having something at my house this Friday and wanted to invite you and of course Sloan and Tiny. It's mostly swim team folks and a few other new people I've met at the swim club. You three will probably be my only non-swimmer guests. So I'm begging for you to come and round the guest list out. I don't want to talk about swimming all night:) And well, I'd really like to see you again. So let me know. It's potluck but you don't have to bring anything. A lot of my friends will bring enough food to feed an army.

-Jagger

It must be divine intervention.

It has to be the universe's way of sending me a lifeline to climb out of the Roman Masterson sinkhole that I'm finding myself falling deeper into every single day.

This time I'm going to grab hold of the lifeline for dear life.

I barely say three words to Roman as we exit the plane, and he says even less. It feels awkward, especially because of what we just shared in my hotel room just hours ago, on top of the fact that I was just starting to get used to his crazy ass. And not just amazing in bed Roman, but the person he is out of bed as well.

He's definitely a lot different than what I'm used to. He's quick-tempered and a loose cannon, but he's also smart, driven, and pays actual attention to me when I'm talking; although I'm pretty sure he's mostly interested in what's between my legs.

I don't think Roman has ever had a serious relationship with a woman, and frankly why would he? Women drool all over him twenty-four hours a day. Why would he pick just one? Particularly one he's related to. Not to mention that I haven't forgotten what he said about not doing seconds. I'm pretty sure the only reason why he's touched me more than once is because I'm living in his father's house.

I'm easy access. Plain and simple.

I'd be kidding myself if I were to think that it's

anything deeper than that. That's what I have to keep remembering. That's what I have to keep telling myself.

When I disembark the plane, Roman is about two people behind me, but I can still feel his Darth Vader-esque eyes drilling holes into the back of my head. Jerk.

"Bitsy!"

I hear the calling of my name rise above a sea of strange faces, before I can locate the direction that it's coming from. That is until I see the white poster board with black lettering being held high by a pair of hands with a big gold love knot ring on one hand. I'd know that ring anywhere; and the words on the sign, well those can only belong to the same person as well.

Welcome Home School Bucks Bitch!

Sure enough I spot Sloan's sun-kissed daddy long legs coming towards me. She's dressed in a casual fitted black T-shirt and a pair of daisy duke jean shorts, looking fabulous as usual, and laughing at the look that's probably plastered across my face after seeing her sign. She's my biggest fan, but she can be a tad bit inappropriate and over the top sometimes.

"Playing hooky?" I ask.

"It's Monday. No doctor wants to be bothered with a pharmaceutical rep on a Monday; that's why I usually do paperwork. But instead I thought I'd pick up the new dot com diva from the airport."

I laugh at the dot com reference because Sloan has no understanding of terminology for websites versus apps, or maybe she just doesn't care, but that's part of her charm. She's a sales powerhouse, a bombshell, daughter of a retired NBA basketball player dad and a voiceover actress mom; and her life's motto is definitely keep it simple stupid. She's not into the minute details of life. She never sweats the small stuff. She just likes good food, hot sex, and getting paid.

"How did you even know what time to pick me up crazy girl?" I ask.

Sloan gestures her head at something or rather someone behind me. "Batman over there sent me a text. Said you'd be needing a ride."

I turn to look for Roman and see that he's not even paying us any attention. He's deeply engrossed in some sort of flirtatious conversation with a red head dressed in an airline uniform. My stomach turns a bit. I'm so sick of him.

"How thoughtful of him," I say snidely.

"Do you have all your things?" Sloan asks. "Do we need to go to baggage claim?"

"No, I didn't check any bags. I just have my carry-on. We can go."

"Cool, let's go then. I've got an Uber car waiting."

I take one last glance over at Roman. For a moment I wish it were he and I traveling in the car home together. Laughing. Flirting. But he's doing both of those things with someone else. A complete stranger. At least I think she's a stranger. Knowing that asshole, she may be someone he may have slept with in the past. I'm sure the list is a mile long.

Ugh, I can't stand him.

"Let's go." I march to the exit door.

During the car ride home Sloan starts rattling off information like I've been away for a month instead of forty-eight hours. She shares celebrity gossip, college friend gossip, work gossip and something about her cable guy. I just didn't hear it all. My mind has been completely zoned out and on you know who.

"So?" Sloan asks while nudging my shoulder with hers.

"What?" I ask.

"I read your letter. Are you ready to talk about it?"

"Oh that."

"So you fooled around with the Dark Knight, huh?"

"Yes," I admit quietly.

"Don't be embarrassed about it with me. I mean he is your cousin, but not really, so I sort of get it."

"You do?" I ask.

"I mean I'm not saying it's the smartest move on your part, but he's super hot, so I get why you may have had a little slip."

"Yes … a little slip."

Sloan starts grinning. "A big slip?"

"Maybe." I shrug my shoulders.

"How big? Did you fuck him?" Her eyes grow wide like saucers as she asks loudly enough for the entire city to hear.

"Yes," I whisper when I notice the Uber guy's eyes on me.

"More than once?"

"Yes."

"Dare I ask because you really have no frame of reference, but was it good."

"Very." I smile.

"So that's why things were so awkward back there. You guys didn't want to share a car because you were a little embarrassed about all the frolicking you've been doing?"

I sigh. "I guess that's part of it."

"Did Joseph send him to keep an eye on you or something? Why was he even there?"

I dodge giving the real answer by side tracking her with half the truth.

"Ethan was there."

"WHAT!"

"My phone was acting funky, or I would have called

you, but I was at the bar having a drink and there he was. He simply walked up to me like it was just another day. Like we had just spoken to each other yesterday."

"WHAT!"

"Yep."

"So what did he say?"

"Well not much. I didn't really give him an opportunity to talk that much. He wasn't in Arizona though or rehab. I'm not sure he's even got a drug problem, Sloan. I don't know what's real and what isn't with him."

"That asshole. I thought he was cool."

"I know."

"So how did you end things? I mean like what did you say? I know he was the love of your life, Bitsy."

That's overstating things a bit.

"Well Roman kind of forced the issue."

"Roman was at the bar with you?"

"No he came by my room."

"Oh so Ethan was in your room?"

"Yep."

"You know I'm looking at your face right now, and I feel like I'm missing something."

"What? I told you the biggest secret I've got."

"Not just that. I feel like you've been holding out on me. Like you're keeping stuff from me."

"Can't a girl keep a few things to herself?"

"Yeah, I guess, but I just don't want to be the last to know. You know how I am."

"I get it. Oh, I didn't get a chance to tell you that Jagger emailed me too."

"Oh?" She says excitedly. "To invite you to the shindig no doubt."

"Uh huh."

"Are you going? I mean it seems like your dance card is super full." She chuckles.

"Ha, ha, very funny."

"I mean ex-boyfriends and cousins—"

The Uber guy looks up at us again through the rear view mirror and grins.

"Would you shut your trap!" I fuss. Then we both start laughing hysterically.

"I mean what's your secret? Do I need to shave my legs or something?"

I start bopping her on her head with my handbag. "Enough crazy girl. I've made my decision. Ethan doesn't exist. Roman was a mistake. And Jagger ... well he's a possibility."

Sloan smiles in approval.

"Well then to Jagger and School Bucks," she says.

And we mock toast each other with our fists like we've done since we were eighteen years old.

"To Jagger and School Bucks."

9

Elizabeth

"I'M SORRY BUT DO your aunt and uncle not allow phone calls inside of the house now? Did they confiscate your cell phone? Are you on some sort of lock down?"

"Very funny, Mother. I'm literally cracking up."

"It's been five days since you've returned from your vacation–"

"My business trip," I correct her but she ignores me as usual.

"And not even a phone call to me or your father. He'd like to speak to you by the way. Your father."

I find that ironic seeing as how I can count on my hand the number of times over six years that my father actually picked up the phone to call me himself. My mother has always been the unofficial spokesperson of the two. Dad always plays the background. Never initiating much contact with me. I know that it doesn't say anything in particular about how much he loves me; it's just his way.

"I'm sorry, Mom. You're right I should have called, but I've been busy. Put Dad on the phone please."

I hear the deep voice that immediately makes me feel five years old again.

"Elizabeth."

"Hi Dad."

"What are you up to, kiddo?" That's a loaded question.

"You know … this and that."

"Do you need money?"

Straight to the point huh. "No, Dad, I'm okay."

"And just what does that mean– okay?"

"Well my business is generating a decent amount of money for me every month." Ok that's actually stretching the truth by leaps and bounds.

"And I'm going to start looking for a job as well."

I came to that revelation on the flight home. If I'm going to successfully stay from underneath Roman's watch, I'm going to have to move out of my aunt's house. There's just no other way.

"So you're staying in the city then?" Disapproval oozing through the phone.

"Yes, Dad."

"And your aunt and uncle, how long are you planning on staying with them?"

"I'm not sure." I huff. Even though I plan on leaving as soon as I can, my father is making me feel like I am some sort of nuisance.

There's a long pause between us, and I know what's coming next. My parents have made their feelings quite apparent to me. They want me home.

"Listen, Bitsy, I definitely want you to chase your dreams, but there's also reality to consider. You can't live off your aunt and uncle forever. It was never supposed to be a permanent arrangement."

"It's not, Dad." If only he knew how much in agreement we are.

"You can live with us and still work on your business. I can even get you a part time job at the courthouse, so you'll have your own spending money."

Oh brother.

"That sounds like a good plan, Dad, but just not the right one for me. Not right now. I love living in the city."

"Elizabeth, I've allowed you to handle things in regards to your assault because you're a grown woman now, but I need to know the truth. Are you in any further danger? Was this really a random incident? I need to know that you're okay. I need to make sure that you aren't keeping anything from me and your mother."

"I'm fine, Dad. Aunt Juliette's house is in a great neighborhood, and I feel completely safe here. Plus when I get a job and it's time for me to move somewhere, I'm pretty sure that Uncle Joseph and Roman will run a check on the landlord and scout the neighborhood like they're CIA," I chuckle.

A pregnant pause passes between us.

"Roman?"

"Yes ... Uncle Joseph's son."

"He's living there?"

Don't he and my mother talk at all?

"No he has his own place, but he works for Uncle Joseph, so I see him here and there."

And every frackin' where.

"I definitely want you out of that house sooner rather than later, Elizabeth." There's a severity in his voice that wasn't there before.

"Why?" I want out too, but not because my father is holding some grudge from a zillion years ago. "Because Roman buried me in the backyard when we were practically toddlers? That's ridiculous, Dad."

"It has nothing to do with that juvenile prank. It's

because I know things about that family that you don't know." My father's voice starts to rise. "And from what I've heard, Roman is very much like his father. They're dangerous people, Elizabeth, and they don't follow rules. They make their own. Those types of people are always dangerous. Family or not."

"They've been nothing but good to me, Dad."

"If I front you six months worth of rent for a new apartment would you move?"

Does he know that I'm sleeping with my "dangerous" cousin or am I just paranoid right now?

"Dad, I'm not going to take your money. Let me figure this thing out on my own. Let me be an adult."

My father sighs in defeat. There's no disputing the whole let me be responsible argument. I've won this round.

"All right, Bitsy. Just be careful."

"Can I ask you something, Dad?"

"Anything."

"What makes Uncle Joseph so dangerous? And if he is such a threat, why did mom suggest for me to stay here in the first place?"

"Regardless of how I feel about her husband, I know that my sister would never let anything happen to you. That's the only reason why you're still there. Let's leave it at that."

"Fine."

"I'm putting your mom back on the phone now. She's chomping at the bit to find out about your trip."

"Okay, Dad. Bye."

"Bye, kiddo."

Tonight is the party at Jagger's and at this point I'm running a little late. I run a little smoothing serum through my curls while I finish my conversation with my mother. We talk for about ten more minutes about my pitch meeting, the weather in the Bahamas, and if I'm seeing anyone special.

I told her that Ethan and I broke up a while ago but obviously never gave her the details as to why, so as far as she's concerned I'm on the open market. I swear my mother could set back the women's liberation movement a hundred years with her ridiculous need to set me up with someone.

I'm sitting on the edge of my bed and fingering through a few of my curls while staring in the mirror. Every time I reach the end of one strand, I think about Roman and how he loves to play with my hair. In fact, for the past few days, almost everything I see or do in this house reminds me of Roman.

I've been shamelessly looking for him to come through the front door everyday since we've returned from the Bahamas, and every day he doesn't. Earlier today I finally broke down and sent him a text.

It was a mistake.

Me: Hey

Roman: What's up?

Me: Where have you been?

Roman: Working

Me: Umm … are we okay?

Roman: Yep

Me: All right then. I'll see you later.

Roman: Cool

His monosyllabic answers felt like tiny little needles pricking at my heart. He is obviously still angry with me for shutting him down and it hurts like hell. It was my fault though. I let things go way too far and then ran away. Once again.

Of course the next obvious thing for us to do was to have sex after all those orgasms he tortured me with. Why wouldn't he think that I would want that? Why wouldn't he be mad that I didn't? I'm ridiculous, and even I know it. Why can't I leave this man alone? Why can't I just worry about School Bucks and finding a part time job? Why can't I get my act together? I'm a hot mess.

But Roman is my weakness.

He's frackin' irresistible.

Just like a Hershey bar … I took a couple of real yummy bites and then realized at the last minute that I was about to eat the whole damn candy bar. So I stopped myself. And even though it hurts like hell right now, I know it was the right thing to do.

So no more indulgences for me anymore. I'm totally off chocolate, and I'm going to stick to my very simple vanilla plan.

1. Go to Jagger's. Have fun at Jagger's. Nice and easy. Safe and simple. No more slippery, slimy Ethan. No more toxic-for-me Roman.

2. Find a job so I can move out of Roman's house.

3. Find an angel investor for School Bucks.

Easy peasy.

I've got this.

Jagger lives in a very modest one bedroom apartment above a dry cleaner close to campus. It's a total jock apartment. Not many furnishings, a desk from IKEA, and not so great lighting, but it's perfect for a get together. Lot's of room for people to mill about, eat, and even dance.

He's invited a few more people than he led me to believe that he knew. I guess I forgot just how popular Jagger used to be in school. The whole swim team is here. The ones from school (that kind of don't talk to me anymore) and some of his new friends he's made over at the swim club. There seem to be a lot of swimmer groupies here as well. Mini skirts up to their eyeballs. Shirts cut low down to their knees. Sloan has been cracking jokes about them ever since we crossed Jagger's threshold.

"There should be a five slut maximum at these things," Sloan says loudly enough for one of the sluts to hear.

"What do you care?" I say embarrassed for whoever is eavesdropping. "You don't even mess with jocks."

"You're right I don't. My dad's bad behavior set me straight on that, but that doesn't mean I want to stare at tits and ass all night."

Jagger approaches us with two mixed drinks in his hands.

"Ladies." He grins.

"Hi there." We both smile.

"Glad you two could make it. Where's Tiny?"

"She had a date. She sends her regrets."

"Cool." Jagger gives me a sweeping once over as he hands me a red plastic cup.

"What's this?" I ask.

"Cosmo's. Made them myself. Is that okay?"

"Yep." I take a sip. "Yum it's good … and a little strong." I say jokingly, but not really. It is a frackin' strong drink.

"You look really pretty tonight, Elizabeth."

"Thank you." I blush.

Jagger looks good too, but I find myself mentally comparing him to Roman in almost every way and unfortunately he isn't stacking up. His height (Roman is way taller), his smile, his voice (Roman's is definitely deeper), his mannerisms. None of them can hold a candle to Roman's. None of them make me tingle from the inside out like Roman's do.

Even down to the drink.

Jagger made me a really good cosmopolitan in a red cup, which I appreciate, but Roman would have asked me what I wanted first, and then he would have made sure it was presented to me in a pretty glass. It would have probably been wine, and then he would have given me a very slow and lazy kiss so that he could taste the wine himself right off of my tongue.

One is still a boy and the other is very much a man. One is so laid back I wonder if he's passionate about anything other than swimming. The other is so intense that I wonder if he can even sleep at night with all the things running around in that head of his.

I've got to stop this.

This type of thinking is self-sabotage, Elizabeth.

Then as if my moment of weakness is some sort of Masterson beacon, he calls, and like the dummy I am … I answer. I answer because I'm so frackin' excited that he's calling me and not the other way around. That maybe he's no longer angry with me. I answer because it's what I always do.

He calls and I come running.

I excuse myself from my conversation with Jagger and Sloan, and step inside what appears to be Jagger's bedroom to take the call privately. Which is a whole weird dynamic in and of itself. Me talking to Roman while sitting on Jagger's bed. I feel a tad bit guilty. For what I don't know. I haven't even done anything yet.

"Hello?"

"What's all that noise?"

"Well hello to you too."

"Where are you, Elizabeth?"

"I'm out with friends?"

"What friends?"

I sigh in annoyance. "The same ones I always hang out

with. What do you want?"

"I want you to come over to my apartment right now."

"No. I'm out and if this isn't an emergency we can talk later."

"I'm sorry." He says in the deepest but most subdued tone I've ever heard from him.

"What?"

"I'm sorry. I've been an asshole all week, but I've only been punishing myself. I need to apologize to you properly. Will you let me come pick you up?"

I want to say yes, dammit! I want to say yes so badly.

"I don't think–"

Suddenly Jagger pops his head inside.

"You all right, Elizabeth? You want another drink?"

I try holding the phone down and to the side of my body without disconnecting Roman, but I'm sure that he can still hear something.

"No I'm still drinking this one." I try to answer quietly. "I'll be out in a second."

Jagger takes a quick glance at the phone in my hand. "Cool."

When he closes the door back, it's only then I pick the cell back up and put it to the side of my face.

"Hello?"

"Please tell me you're not with a fucking man."

"I'm not with a man. I'm out with friends."

"So the pretty boy swimmer is there? Because that's exactly who it sounded like just now."

I hesitate for a moment. "Yes, it was Jagger."

I hear an assortment of muffled expletives.

"Where. The. Fuck. Are. You?"

"Roman."

"Where? I'm coming to get you now."

"No."

"What the fuck did you just say?"

"Stop cursing at me asshole. You're not just going to call me after five days of you putting me on some sort of Masterson time out and think you can just bully your way into wrecking my evening, because you feel the need to apologize right this minute. You apologize when I'm ready to hear the damn apology and not a frackin' minute sooner! Do you understand Neanderthal?"

"Duchess—"

"I'll call you when I'm ready to talk *cousin*."

Click.

10

Roman

"SO IS THE MENDEZ problem taken care of?"

I hear the thunderous noise of someone's palm banging on the table; breaking through my haze of pure internal rage. I want to kill Elizabeth Hill, and then I want to fuck the shit out of her or vice-versa.

She's made her point loud and fucking clear.

I haven't been able to catch her at the house for three days and it's making me start to think really crazy shit. I even spent the night there one night, and she didn't come home. The nerve of her little ass. If I don't find her today, I may have Cutter put a tail on that Jagger kid. She's got to show up at some point and if it's with him, I'm going to beat his ass and make her watch.

"Roman!"

"Yes," I hiss.

"Did you take care of the Mendez doctor?" Camden asks me with a what-the-fuck face.

"Obviously."

"What was his price?"

"He didn't have a price. He had a breaking point."

"Understood."

"What's up with the clubs?" I ask Cutter trying to get my head back into this meeting.

"Good. New York and Philly are on track. I may have to go down to Miami and get things in order down there."

"And the DUI, Cam?"

"Handled and expunged. Fucking sexy ass lawyer handled it too."

"Cool. Listen, I know my father said that he had all the players handled in this Mendez gig, but this one is big money for us. He's going to get the fee that he charged Mendez, but the three of us are going to get the backend. A portion of his endorsement money. That's long and solid. So I want to double check that everyone stays silent like they're supposed to. I don't want any surprises the day of his interview. If there's even a peep of anyone talking to the press, the deal is dead for us. You feel me?"

"On it. I'll start checking everyone on the list again," Camden says. "No mistakes."

"Hey Rome let me chat with you a minute," Jade interrupts.

"Okay, Kings, we're done."

"And would you please get some ass tonight. You've been acting like a real bitch for days," Cutter teases.

I slap him upside his head.

"Shut up, dickhead."

Both brothers chuckle at my expense as they exit the room.

"So what's up?" I ask Jade. "Did you find her?"

Instead of using ball-busting Cutter, I decided to put my little Chihuahua on the job. How hard can it be to track down one woman? A woman who lives in my father's house for God's sake.

"Does your cousin know that you own the Red Raisin?"

"I don't think so."

"Well that friend of hers, Sloan, made a reservation for four there tonight. I only know because I dropped by there and saw her making a reservation with Renee. The chances are probably pretty good that Elizabeth may be one of those four."

"Sounds like a fucking date night," I practically growl.

Jade shrugs her shoulders. "Maybe, maybe not, but at least you know there's a chance you can find her there. So my job is done?"

"Yeah."

"Oh, there's also something else you should know."

"What now?"

"The ex is back in town."

"Back where?"

Jade hesitates to answer me.

"Where, Jade?"

"I need to know what you are going to do first? He didn't do anything to Elizabeth in the Bahamas but talk to her."

"I think you're very much confused. Since when is it any of your concern how I handle my business?"

"It usually isn't, but I'm making it my business today. Leave him alone. Leave her alone. In fact leave all of this shit alone, Roman. You're acting like a teenaged, pimply faced, pussy-whipped kid when it comes to her. You're not acting like yourself. I don't have anything against her, but she's your cousin, not your girl. If you keep this up people are going to find out and then what?"

But that's the thing.

"I don't give a shit if people find out anymore."

I finally fucking see her.

In the parking lot of the Red Raisin and she's alone. She's more beautiful than she was just a few days ago, and my hard as a rock dick seems to be in agreement. She notices my presence almost immediately, and if I'm not mistaken by the look on her face, she seems petrified. What I'd like to know is if she's frightened of me or actually of herself.

"Did you need something, Roman?" She asks with a sarcastic twang; trying very hard to be a badass.

So fucking cute.

"You haven't been taking my calls, Elizabeth."

I can't help but smirk while I step in closer to her and when I do, I get a whiff of the Jasmine shower gel she uses everyday. I want to run my nose all up and down the side of her neck, and burrow it in her chest, but I can't let her sweet ass distract me right now.

"I can't do this with you, Roman."

"Do what?" I step in even closer.

"This. It's too much. You're ... too much."

Just one whiff is all I want.

Then maybe one taste.

Suddenly I'm not as angry as I was. Suddenly I just want her, on all fours, moaning my name.

"Sometimes I feel like I can't breathe when you're around, Roman. It's almost as if you control me. Like you own me. And I don't know when it all happened."

She tries to back away from me, but I continue to move forward. I won't let her run from me again. Not again. Especially after what she's just said to me.

"No, Duchess, don't you get it yet? You own me."

As I move her further backwards, she bumps into the brick wall of The Red Raisin. I place one of my palms flat on the wall above her head, and then use my other hand to drape around her waist. I do this all in silence as I wait for her to continue saying what she needs to say to me.

She's staying tight lipped for now, so I continue to talk, while I begin petting the tops of her breasts. I don't give a shit that we're in a public parking lot. Right now it's just the two of us. No one else matters until I say what I need to say.

I want to tell her that I think she's one of the most fascinating women I've ever met. I want to show her in this badly lit parking lot just how much I want inside of her. But I know that all of that would send her running further away from me than she already is. And I can't have that. Not anymore. I'm tired of that shit.

"What are you afraid of, Elizabeth?"

I continue to stroke and pet her breasts with the front and backs of my fingers. I brush one of her nipples once, then again, and then stop to give it a firm tweak with two of my fingers. Her tits are my second favorite body part on Elizabeth (second only to that ass), especially because of how responsive she is when I suck them, touch them or even talk about them.

"I'm asking again, baby. What are you afraid of?"

"I'm afraid of this … whatever this is that is drawing us towards each other. I'm afraid of you."

"You think I don't know why you keep running to that pretty boy Jagger? Don't you think I want to be the safe, boring, dependable man that you seem to think you so desperately need? But I'm not that man, Elizabeth, and I will never be. I'm a lot of not-so-nice shit, Elizabeth, and I'm your cousin, there's no changing any of that. But so the fuck what.

"Because I know without a doubt that I may not be who you think you want, but I'm what you need. I see it when I look at you, feel it when I hold you, and I'm sure as fuck of it when I'm inside you and you come for me."

I watch her eyes glaze over in response to everything I've just said. One thing about Elizabeth fucking Hill is that she's so responsive to my touch and my words. I love it. What man wouldn't love this in his bed every night? What man wouldn't fight for this woman to be in his bed every fucking night?

"You want to come for me right now don't you, Elizabeth."

I've been caressing and petting her for going on ten minutes now, and I'd bet the farm that her panties are soaking wet.

"You can't do that."

"Is that a challenge, baby?"

"No, it's just … we're outside, Roman."

"You want to get in my car?"

"No!"

"Okay then, you must want to come right here in this parking lot."

"For God's sake."

"Whose sake, baby?"

I pull her scoop necked T-shirt a little further down and pop one of her breasts out of her bra. Her areola tightens and her nipple pebbles as soon as the crisp air hits it. Her left breast is my favorite of the two. So sensitive and tender. Now I think it's time I show Elizabeth just how much I favor it.

"Roman–"

"Who?" I tease.

"Masterson."

"Aah, that's my girl. Now since we're in a public place and my girl won't get in the car, I'm just going to have to make you come with all of your clothes on right against this wall."

Elizabeth raises one of her eyebrows in what seems like skepticism.

"You don't believe that I posses such skills do you?"

"No," she giggles. One of my favorite sounds.

"Let me show you."

I surprise Elizabeth when I lift her up.

"Wrap your legs around my waist."

She hesitates for a moment.

"Now Duchess."

She takes a sweeping glance across the parking lot while I lift her up. People are slowly beginning to pull in to park, and I suspect she's looking for Sloan and whoever else they're planning on eating with tonight, but I don't give a shit. What I need is for her to get her head back into this right here. Us.

I latch my mouth onto her left breast and suck strongly until I feel her body tighten, then I release and start swirling my tongue around her nipple. I continue this rhythm of sucking and swirling until her breaths become shallow and she starts arching her back to give me more of what I want. That's when I know I have her full attention.

"Give me the other," I demand and she does without hesitation.

She slides the front of her top down further and pops out the other breast. The right one is fuller than the left. Her nipple is puffier. This one can take a little more abuse without it being painful; and it's my knowledge of what each of her tits need from me that's going to set her off and explode for me in about five more minutes.

I keep alternating sucking, swirling and gently blowing across Elizabeth's nipples while she starts to writhe around my waist. I make sure that my hands are kneading her ass in the same rhythm that I'm sucking her breasts. I look up for a moment to check her expression and notice that her cheeks are flushed, her eyes closed, and her lips are slightly parted.

She's ready.

I slap the side of her ass hard with one of my hands while still holding her up with the other.

"Running from me won't work, Duchess."

She moans.

Now that I've stopped sucking her breasts, I start grinding her against the wall. Making sure that my length rubs directly against the top of her clit where she likes it. My dick fits perfectly in between her legs. Like a dog that's finally found a soft, warm place that feels like home. I could stay the fuck here forever.

"Running from me will never work. I'll just fucking find you."

I slap her ass again. Thanks to her jeans it's not the usually loud, cracking sound that I take pleasure in hearing when it's just the two of us, naked and alone. But it will do. Her breaths are getting even quicker. She's almost there.

"Whose ass is this, Duchess?"

Her face contorts. I love this shit. She's ready to blow.

I take a hard pull of her right breast with my mouth like I'm hitting a joint. Then I hit her ass again with full force. That's when she lets out a yelp that I smother with my smile. I pull back and whisper something in her ear that I know will end all this shit right now.

"I should bend you over one of these cars and fuck the shit out of you in front of all of these people for not answering me the first time. You want me to do that, Duchess? 'Cause I fucking will. Don't test me."

I hold her up against the wall with my body weight and

take my hands and pinch both of her nipples at the same time.

"Look at me," I order.

Her head snaps up. Breathless. Flushed. So fucking beautiful.

"Whose. Ass. Is. This?"

"Yours."

And then she explodes while chanting my name like a prayer.

"It's yours, Masterson."

And I know from this day on that I'll do whatever I have to do to keep hearing that plea from her lips for the rest of my life.

11

Elizabeth

I'M ANNOYED WITH MYSELF.

I ended up bailing on dinner with Sloan, Jagger, and some new guy she met, because I was getting turned the hell out by my stalker a.k.a. Roman all frackin' night. When it became obvious that I couldn't go inside the Red Raisin and have dinner with another man looking freshly fucked (well sort of), I basically acquiesced and went home with Roman for a continued romp and subsequent punishment for my "disappearing act".

Instead of death by orgasm though, he executed a different type of penalty. This time it was death by *no* orgasm. He literally brought me to the edge of coming about seven different times, in seven very creative ways, and then stopped every single time.

It was the meanest thing ever.

I was sopping wet, completely frustrated and definitely unsatisfied. I got so angry that I actually starting tearing up. Not that the Neanderthal cared.

Right now the orgasm bully is downstairs eating some sort of late breakfast that Juliette's whipped up for him. I know that he's just killing time waiting for me to come downstairs though. So I'm trying my best to wait him out up here, because my worst fear is that my aunt or uncle will pick up on the sexual energy that bounces off of the walls whenever the two of us are in a room together.

Hell, I think it's only getting worse.

Of course Roman doesn't give a crap whether they see it or not. I'm starting to really understand that about him. He thinks this is one big game with little to no consideration of what the ramifications are for me and my family.

Jackass.

A rare, soft double knock on my door lets me know that it's my uncle.

I crack the door open. "Hey."

"Hi, Elizabeth." He looks at me and then around my room. "You up here working or are you headed out?"

"I'm headed out actually. I was thinking of looking for a part time job until things pick up for my app."

He raises his eyebrows.

"Do you want a part time job?"

I don't know exactly what he means by that question. "Yes, I need a job."

"I can give you a little money to hold you over until things pick up, darlin'. What do you need? A stack?"

What's a stack again? A thousand dollars?

"Umm, no thank you, Uncle Joseph. You giving me room and board are enough. You've done so much for me already."

"Are you comfortable living here, Elizabeth?"

"Yes, of course."

"You aren't thinking about moving out just yet are you?"

Jeez. He's like a mind reader or something.

"Umm, well I've been giving it some thought. I can't stay here forever right?" I smile brightly.

"You just got here."

Based on my uncle's strained expression, I'm wondering if I've just offended him in some way.

"I'm not moving tomorrow," I nervously chuckle. "I'm just trying to get all my ducks in a row. That's all."

"Is Roman bothering you?"

"Absolutely not!"

My uncle stares at me quietly. I think I may have just messed up. *I fear the lady doth protest too much.*

"Juliette whipped up one of her famous breakfast quiches," he says. "Why don't you have a slice before you head out?"

I know that's an order and not a request.

Like father like son.

"Okay, I'll be down in a few, Uncle J. Just straightening up in here."

"Okay, darlin'."

So ... I'm still annoyed with myself.

Since I know that I'm about to see Roman, like a nut ball I decide against wearing my blue power suit and change into a pair of steel gray skinny jeans, a pale gray cami top, a charcoal blazer on top, and a pair of my favorite black pumps. The jeans are super tight since I've gained at least three pounds by eating stuff like Aunt Juliette's famous quiche. So I know that Roman's going to love them, because if there's one thing about him that I know for sure, it's that he loves staring at and touching my ass.

I know ... I'm ridiculous right now. I can't even stand myself.

"Morning, Elizabeth!" Juliette says in the bubbliest tone ever. She must be one of the happiest people I've ever met in my entire life. I can't believe we're actually related.

"Morning, babe," she says a little softer to Uncle Joseph as he strides over and pulls Juliette into his arms.

"Morning," he says nuzzling her neck while smacking her gently on the ass.

Oh brother.

Definitely like father, like son.

"Morning," I mumble back to Juliette trying desperately to avoid the smirk spread across Roman's face at how uncomfortable I am.

"All dressed up and nowhere to go?" Roman says to me instead of good morning.

"Elizabeth is going job hunting," Joseph interjects.

"Is that right?"

Roman slowly drags his gaze up and down my body, and I already can tell that he's thinking about sabotaging my day.

"You're going to look for a job dressed like that?"

"I think she looks pretty," Juliette interjects.

"Thanks, Auntie." I smirk.

"I didn't say that she didn't look pretty," Roman says.

The room grows so silent you could hear a pin drop. I could literally wring his neck right now.

"So what are you saying then?" Juliette asks a little perplexed while Joseph quietly observes the both of us.

"I'm saying that the last time I checked wearing tight pants to go on a job interview wasn't professional."

"I'm not interviewing at The White House," I raise my voice sarcastically. "I'm trying to get a job waitressing or something."

Roman turns to Uncle Joseph. "You approve of this?"

"You don't?" My uncle asks incredulously, waiting for Roman's response.

This is going downhill fast.

I'm so out of here.

"Auntie, where is this quiche everyone's been talking about. I'd like a slice before I head out."

"Oh sure, sweetie. Sit down. Let me warm you up a slice. You want water or orange juice?"

"Water, please." I take a quick glance at Roman, while Uncle Joseph is distracted by my aunt's behind, and beg him with my eyes to sit down and shut up.

Finally he sits.

"I have a friend who's a manager over at The Four Seasons, Elizabeth. I can give him a call," Uncle Joseph says to me. "There's no need for you to go every which where. Plus filling out applications is mostly done online now anyway. Not too many places are going to let you walk in and fill out an application on site anymore."

What my uncle is saying makes total sense and is definitely the smarter way to go, but The Four Seasons sounds like a *real* job. One that might interfere with me building my business. I need more flexibility if I'm really going to make my business work.

"Umm ... I'm not sure about The Four Seasons, Uncle Joseph."

"Well how about this. You know computers right?"

"Sure."

"How about you set up a network for us in all of the clubs? I'd like for all of the computers to be able to talk to one another, and I've been meaning to get it done for the longest time. Our computer system is really outdated. I hate having to call and get stats from every individual manager. I'd rather check everything myself in one database. You can hire someone to help you if you need it, but just one person."

"Uh, should you and I have a discussion about this?" Roman interrupts.

"About what? You need it done and your cousin can do it. What's to discuss?"

Roman abruptly stands up from his chair.

"It's my decision to make."

"Sit down, boy. You're in my kitchen and the decision is already made. I haven't given you shit quite yet. At least not until the lawyers send back the paperwork."

"Joseph Michael Masterson! There's no need to talk to your son using that language in my kitchen," Juliette admonishes.

"Oh my God," I say. "I don't even want the job. So everyone calm down."

"Why not?!" Roman turns his head and barks at me like the complete psycho he is. Wasn't he just about to argue his father down that he didn't want me taking this job?

"I could NEVER work for you. You are a complete crazy person. I'm sorry, Uncle Joseph, but I cannot work for this nut job."

"How about we all make an agreement then," Juliette adds with a little chuckle to her voice. "You only work in a location when Roman's not in the building. If he's at The Lotus that day, then you work at Solstice. And so on and so forth. He doesn't need to be around when you're working on the computers right?"

"What?!" Roman yells angrily.

"Simmer down," Joseph warns. "And don't you ever raise your voice to my wife again."

I know that Roman didn't mean to yell at Juliette, and Juliette knows it too; but I can see that Joseph is deadly serious. He's not loud at all. Not like Roman. He has more of a deadly calm demeanor that in my opinion takes years of practice to master. It's the type of calmness that reminds me of why my father may mistrust him.

Whatever he is though, what I do know is that he loves the hell out of my aunt, and I really like him for that. I guess sometimes he's just over the top with his protectiveness of her.

"I'm sorry, Juliette."

"It's no problem, sweetie. Joseph was simply overreacting as usual." My aunt clunks down a plate of quiche in front of Joseph and practically tosses a fork in his lap.

"Listen … I think that the two of you can work out your own sensible working relationship that doesn't require an entire family discussion over breakfast. You're the boss, Roman. Just don't be so temperamental with Elizabeth okay?" My aunt winks at me.

I think I catch my uncle rolling his eyes at one of us, or all of us while he begins eating his slice of spinach and bacon quiche. He seems to be finished with the conversation as much as I am, and I almost feel as though Roman and I have been unceremoniously dismissed by him.

I swear that he and Roman have such a weird dynamic.

"Finish up your food and let's go." Roman says to me.

"Where are we going?"

I'm not sure what I'm doing at this point. Am I going to still go job hunting? Should I really do this computer thing for them? I mean it was Joseph asking me to do it, and I'm sleeping in his damn house rent-free. So maybe I should.

"To finish having a sensible discussion about how you're going to build us a network."

"Why can't we finish having our discussion here?" I ask.

Roman gives me the side eye before he responds.

"How can you make a decision on whether or not you want the job if you haven't even seen what it entails. I'm taking you by the clubs to see the computers."

"Oh that's a good idea, Roman," my aunt says in a lighter tone.

She's back to flittering around the kitchen, wiping the counters, and pouring herself a glass of grapefruit juice while my uncle watches her ass very, very closely.

Eww.

I can see that it probably may be a good idea to leave, because it seems as if my aunt has some morning sex coming her way in the very immediate future. And I swear she might have a Masterson style punishment coming her way too for interfering in his business with Roman or for throwing that fork at him. Something tells me that father and son are much more alike than I ever imagined.

So on that note, I take my last bite of quiche and excuse myself from the table. After that visual, I'll do anything to get out of here.

"Let's go."

12

Elizabeth

IT'S quiet in the car.

Not because Roman is angry, but because he appears to be thinking very pensively about something. Knowing him … it's probably about how he plans on spreading my legs in the next thirty minutes. Or maybe that's wishful thinking on my part.

"Have you heard anything from the investment group?"

"Not yet."

"The glamazon is dating one of them right?"

"Not exactly. She used to date him."

"And what happened?"

"Well you know who her father is right?"

"Should I?"

"Her last name is Pearson. Her father is Dan Pearson, the famous point guard for the Sixers in the nineties and a few other teams at the tail end of his career."

"I don't follow basketball, but I know who you're talking about. Old dude from back in the day. A commentator on ESPN right?"

"Yes … that old dude," I affirm wryly. "Well the guy in

the investment group seemed to only be dating Sloan to get close to her father. I don't know if he wanted to manage Mr. Pearson's portfolio or if he just has some sort of man crush on him; but as soon as Sloan figured it out, she cut him immediately off."

"Yet he's still helping out by getting you a meeting with his boss?"

"I guess he's trying to earn his way back into her circle of trust."

"Well he's doing a piss poor job at it. Someone should have called you by now."

I sigh.

"It hasn't even been that long, Roman, and it's a big decision. They just can't invest money into every entrepreneur that crosses their path. They have to be selective. While I am hopeful, I didn't even expect to hear from them yet. Mr. Lambert already warned me that it was going to be a lengthy decision process."

"Please." Roman scrunches up the side of his face.

"Why are you being so frackin' negative?"

Roman takes a long pause before he responds. Then he turns to me with a hard lined face. I swear his scar just got bigger.

"Did it ever occur to you to ask me for the fucking money, Elizabeth?"

"Not really."

"You said that real quickly." He begins to mimic my voice. "*Not really.*"

"Are you honestly angry with me right now?" I ask flabbergasted.

"Hell fucking yeah. I don't understand you. If you're a businesswoman, you've made a grave error in not tapping into the resources right under your cute little nose. You'll let me lick that pussy clean, but you won't let me give you a little money to invest in your business?"

My core convulses from his crude choice of words. I hate that I actually want him in between my legs doing just that, right in the middle of him berating me.

"You're being ridiculous right now."

"And what the fuck was up with all of that grand standing in the house?"

"What are you talking about, Roman?"

"You don't want to work for a nut ball? Don't you think you're pouring it on a little too thickly? My father isn't an idiot. This whole I hate Roman act is completely unbelievable. "

"Is it?"

"Don't be a smart ass."

"I can't help it. God gave me this brain."

"God gave you that ass too, but that doesn't mean I won't smack it."

"Like your father did to Juliette today?"

"Thanks. That's a real nice visual, Elizabeth."

I laugh out loud hoping that I can change the mood in the car between us. But he's still wearing that serious face of his.

"Why do you want a job, Elizabeth? I mean why right now?"

"Because some drug dealers stole my entire life savings and I'm broke," I say with sarcasm. "Could that be why?"

"It could be, but it isn't. I'm an expert on runners, Elizabeth. People have been running from me my whole life."

"Because you scare the heck out of people."

He ignores that comment.

"You're running. You think I don't know that you are trying to get your hands on some more money so that you can leave my father's house. So that you don't have to see me everyday. As if that is going to stop a damn thing."

"Since when does looking for a job constitute a frackin' secret mission to get the heck away from you? Everything is not about you, Roman. I know that's hard for you to believe, considering you have women falling all over your ass at any given second but wake up. I'm looking for a job because regular folks need to work to pay bills."

"You think I don't work?!" he barks incredulously.

"I don't know what the frack you do."

"Stop saying that goddamn word!"

Roman slows his Range Rover down and begins to parallel park into a tight spot in front of a storefront with burnt orange fabric awnings that read Solstice in white and pale yellow lettering. It's obvious that it is some sort of restaurant/lounge, but it doesn't seem like a business that Joseph or Roman would own.

It appears to be closed to the public, but I think I see at least one guy inside milling about. Probably the manager.

"Why can't I say *frack*?" I ask as calmly as I can in an effort to piss Roman off even further. And it does.

"Right now I'm going to need you to shut the *frack* up, while I show you the two old ass computers we have in the office of Solstice; which is our tapas lounge by the way. Because if you don't, if you say one more smart ass thing, Elizabeth, I'll fuck you long and hard in that office instead. Loud enough for Jason to hear; and I won't give two shits about it."

"Who's Jason?" I ask in a flirty way. I know I'm skirting the danger zone, but I can't help it. He's making it too easy.

Roman takes several long deep breaths while he begins to slowly eye fuck me. If I don't watch it he's going to bang my brains out right inside the back of this truck on this busy commercial block.

A text comes in on my phone. I break eye contact with Roman to take a short glance at it.

Jagger: You stood me up:(

I look quickly back up at Roman, and he's staring at my fingers resting on the letters of the keyboard of my phone. I look back down and quickly thumb type.

Me: So sorry. Something—

Before I can finish texting my lame excuse about why I left Jagger hanging in the restaurant with Sloan and her boy toy for the evening, Roman snatches the phone away and reads the text.

"Give me my phone back!" I yell as I reach over to grab it from his hand. He raises his arm higher.

"Nope." He grins.

"Stop playing," I argue.

"Nope. Nada. Negative. Uh-uh."

"Roman!"

"I'm going to text him back that you're so sorry, but that you are being so well fucked by your cousin that there's no need to take this shit any further."

He raises his hand higher and out the window. My phone could literally drop on the sidewalk if he slips up, and my screen would shatter into little tiny pieces. He's such a big dang kid.

"Roman, I'm not playing. Give me my phone back. You're such a child sometimes."

"No, baby, I'm all man. You know that better than anyone."

I roll my eyes after he grips his junk.

"It's always sex with you isn't it?"

"What's not to like about sex?"

"It's just a shame that you're so one dimensional."

"What the fuck did you just say?"

It was an intentional jab, but it's the truth. All we have is this fierce sexual chemistry between us with zero substance, because he lacks the ability to think or talk about anything besides sex.

"All you think about is money and sex. Like some sort of rapper or ball player."

"First of all you're making some mighty ignorant and sweeping generalizations of two groups of people, which tells me, *nerd*, that you've had your head in your computer way too long. Secondly, you are very much wrong about me. I'm multi-dimensional and multi-layered. You just don't choose to see it."

"Is that so?"

"That is definitely so, Duchess."

Roman flashes me one of those panty dropping smiles of his that makes me want to spread eagle for him any time, any place, any where.

So annoying.

"In fact, once we spend the next hour or so taking a look at all of our retro computers, I want us to do something a little different today."

"Another job run?" I asked bored.

"Not this time."

"Well what then?"

"We're going to go do one of my favorite things."

"I think we've done that a few times already," I say drolly.

"I said one of them. Not my number one favorite thing."

We both laugh a little.

Then I stop.

Roman is staring at me with those coal black eyes like

he can see straight inside my soul. I look down and away from him. I guess from embarrassment. I don't know what to make of it when he stares me down like this. Like I'm the only woman breathing. I almost want to believe that it really means something, when I already know that it doesn't.

"You look fucking sexy as hell today, Duchess. Did I tell you that?"

Nothing will come out of my mouth, so I shake my head no.

"I can't hear you, baby. I said do you know how fucking sexy you are?"

"Roman," I say in hopes of quieting him.

"Lean over here a minute, Duchess."

I close my eyes for a moment while I exhale. I don't lean over, because I know what's coming next. Right on this busy street inside his car. Either his mouth or his hands. I'm not sure which, but something.

His hands.

He takes one of his massive palms and wraps it around my neck while his thumb gently rubs the hollow point at the base of my throat.

"Since you don't know how to follow fucking directions, I'll help you out," he growls.

He pulls me over to the driver's side of the car with his hand and uses the other to reach inside and underneath my blazer. Caressing the side of my waist.

Like a Pavlovian dog's response, my mouth starts to water, and my breaths start to become quicker and shallower. I want him in the worst frackin' way. I just do. I always do when he touches me.

His grip around my neck is firm and territorial and screams of possession, and that's also exactly the way his kiss feels. His tongue begins a familiar slide inside of my mouth, exploring gently, coaxing me to respond to the rhythm of his dips and swirls.

I don't mean to do it, but a soft moan comes from somewhere inside of me which he seems to really like. I can tell that he is growing hard inside of his jeans. There's that Pavlovian thing again, because now that I know he's hard, I start imagining all sorts of things. Like how hard I would have to work to get that big thing inside of my mouth and work it properly.

Someone suddenly leans on their car horn and the noise scares the bejeezus out of me, and snaps me out of the total mind frack that Roman was putting me in.

"We need to stop," I say as I pull away from his grasp.

"You're right. Let's go inside."

I think Roman has plans on continuing where he left off inside Solstice, but I'm not going to let that happen. I'm here to possibly work, not play around with him all day.

"And give me my phone back."

"Let's come to an understanding first."

"I'm not negotiating with you about my phone. Give it back right the frack now."

"So here's the deal–" He begins. Completely ignoring my last statement.

"I'll give you your phone back under two conditions. Or I don't give you your phone back, and I go through all of your texts and emails and see what kind of mischief I can get into with all of your peeps."

"I'm going to tell Joseph on you."

I'm desperate at this point. I don't want to commit to any sort of compromise agreement with this Neanderthal.

"Go ahead." He leans back into the corner of his seat with a smirk across his face. "Tell him everything. Tell him how just five minutes ago you would have let me do any fucking thing to you in this car, in broad daylight, on one of the busiest streets in the city.

I can't stand him.

"What are the conditions, asshole."

"Asshole? I love it! No weird nerd synonyms for that one huh? Just the good old fashioned ass and hole."

"UGH!" I scream in frustration.

"All right, Duchess. Calm your pretty little ass down. Here's the deal. I want you to go out on a date with me tonight. A real one. After we do some work today, I want to take you back home, then I want you to shower and get all fucking pretty, and let me take you out.

"Second, I want you to call pretty boy and break it to him hard, break it to him gently; hell, I don't give a shit. Just break it to that dickhead that you are not available for late night phone calls and FaceTime chats, for swim meets, for dinner, and for whatever else the fuck that kid wants to do with you. And tell him with me in the room when you do it."

"You must be losing your ever loving mind."

"What?" He shrugs his shoulders.

"You're making the demands of a boyfriend. Or of someone that wants to be my boyfriend, which we know very well that you are not nor ever will be."

"Did I say I wanted to be your boyfriend?"

Now I'm embarrassed. Did I overreact?

"No, but I can't give you what you're asking."

"Why?"

"I can't go on a date with my own frackin' cousin, Roman!"

"So that's the part of this deal that's bothering you?"

"Hell yeah."

"It's not a date then. I just want to take you to see one of my favorite spots in the city. We'll talk. Then we can grab something to eat or we can go home. We're just hanging out. No fucking around."

"No sex?"

"I won't touch you. Plus I want to get tested and assure you that I'm clean before I have you again. Have you the way I really want to. With nothing between us."

"So no sex really?"

"You sound disappointed," he chuckles.

"No … I'm very much fine with that arrangement."

"Okay, good. And the swimmer?"

I exhale slowly before I respond. It's actually pretty cruel for me to keep stringing Jagger along as if I'm really interested in him. I mean I like him a lot, but if I'm going to be really honest with myself, I need to get Roman totally out of my system before I commit to a good guy like Jagger. I don't want to hurt him.

"I'll talk to Jagger, but not on the phone, and not with you in the room. I'm going to meet with him and tell him. He's my friend. Not just some random dude."

"Give me one last kiss since I'm not getting anymore tonight, and I'll agree to that."

This time when we kiss, Roman's hand reaches back inside my blazer and down the back of my jeans. It's a very tight fit, but he manages to shove his hand down there and squeeze one of my butt cheeks.

The minute he squeezes is the minute I feel the gush between my legs.

"Masterson," I whisper.

"Yes, baby?"

"You're confusing the frack out of me."

"I know."

As I continue kissing him, I begin rubbing my hands across his head, because I know he loves this. That's the crazy part about this whole thing. I want to please him. I enjoy it. I'm not sure when that started either.

Then he pulls back and breaks contact.

I'm shocked at first, because I'm always the one to stop (if we stop).

"Let's go inside." He smiles as he motions to exit the truck. "We've got work to do."

13

Roman

I KNOW what I said the other day about doing all that I had to do to keep Elizabeth moaning my name yada, yada, yada; but truthfully I don't know what the fuck I'm doing. Wait, scratch that. I know what the fuck I'm doing; I just don't really understand why I'm doing it.

What's my end game?

It was never my plan or intention to take Elizabeth out on a date.

Ever.

I don't even go on dates. Who has time for that shit? And up until now it hasn't been an issue. There are plenty of women out here who appreciate a good fuck, just like me and don't want to be tied down, I find them all the time for the most part. Sure there may be a few clingy Carols every once in a while, but you're bound to run into a few bad apples here and there.

So the fact that I'm sitting here plotting and planning a night out to woo my cousin is somewhat laughable. No let me rephrase that. It's insane.

We spent the greater part of today visiting all five of the spots Joseph (and I now) own in Philly, and we also called management of the two we own in Manhattan and the one in Miami.

I got brick fucking hard just watching Elizabeth get busy in her element. Inspecting the old ass desktops, asking the manager's questions about the databases and them staring at her like she was speaking another language. It was all some very smarty pants, sexy shit. And it smelled very much like foreplay to me. If I thought she would have been down for it, I would have fucked her silly in every back room of every location we dropped by today.

Maybe I still will.

That little shit Jade hung up on me today. Maybe I pay her too much money. Maybe she isn't desperate enough for a job. That girl needs an attitude adjustment or a month on the unemployment line. That will straighten her ass out real quick. All I did was call her and ask for her help to plan my non-date, and needless to say she wasn't too happy about the request.

"You can't honestly be considering taking Elizabeth out on a date? See this is what I'm talking about when it comes to rich people. You all make so much money that you have no idea what to do with yourselves. You fuck so many random bitches that you're bored, and so now you want to date your own cousin? For what, to spice things up?"

"Simmer the fuck down, munchkin," I warned her.

Of course she wasn't affected at all by my warning. Jade might be one of the only people who isn't intimidated by me. Well her and Elizabeth.

"Then you call me asking me for personal favors and crap. Not asking me about a lick of business. Just more shiznit about Elizabeth. Your couzzzzin."

She exaggerated the word cousin as if I didn't already know how backwater fucked up this is.

"Do I have to explain any further how crazy you sound, Roman?"

I really wanted to reach through the phone and kill her little spitfire ass or at least send Camden to do it, since I suspect that he has some sort of thing for her. He's always staring at her when she isn't looking.

"No little peewee. You don't need to explain any fucking thing, because guess what? I don't give a shit about what you have to say. And yes, I am asking you to do personal stuff for me, because you are a personal assistant in case you didn't realize that shit."

"I'm an executive assistant," she huffed.

"To be an executive assistant you have to be working for executives Einstein. And we are nobody's executives. We shake down people for a living. Plain and simple. And your job is to do whatever the fuck I need to make that happen or anything else I want to happen for that matter. You feel me?"

Jade started popping her gum a little more loudly after I dug into her ass. She was pissed, but she knew I was right and more than that, she knew I was dead ass serious.

There's a time for banter and then there's a time for showing fucking respect to the people who pay you, and she wasn't paying it to me. And I'm not having that shit. I don't care how long the two of us go back.

"What do you need?"

I could have tore into her ass a little further; and if she was anyone else I would have, but then I could hear that *you hurt my feelings* tone in her voice, so I couldn't.

Yep, it's official.

Elizabeth's turned me into a pussy.

Angry with me or not, Jade planned what seems to be like a perfect first date, but not really a date. First, I'm picking Elizabeth up from the house on the pretense that we're going by the Apple Store to look for new computers.

I need Joseph's nosy ass to believe that, so we're going

to have to stop at the one on Walnut Street and buy some shit before we continue on with the rest of our date.

Why the fuck do I keep calling it that?

I call Elizabeth instead of texting her, in order to let her know that I'm five minutes away, because I want her to see the dick shot I took of myself and put in her contacts. The picture will pop up when I call.

Well it's not a literal dick shot, it's just a pic of my hard ass bulge straining to get out of my jeans and into her heavenly pussy. She's going to hate it. Which is exactly what I'm shooting for. She looks so fucking sexy when she's pissed.

"I can't believe you put this shit in my phone," she whispers angrily when she opens the door. The look on her face is so fucking funny; I almost lose my shit on the front stoop.

"I love how I'm rubbing off on you, Elizabeth. You've said two real curse words today. I'm so proud of you baby."

She quickly whips her head around to see if anyone can hear us.

"Stop calling me that," she whispers again.

"They know that I'm coming over, Elizabeth."

"Not for your baby!" she says in her best whisper-scream voice. Hysterically funny.

"You're so fucking cute."

"Let's just go."

It's unusual for Juliette to not come to do the door and say hello regardless of the fact that she's already seen me today. That's just her. All bubbly and shit. It's actually one of the things that my father must find attractive about her. Especially since he's always in a bad-ass mood. He's been an icy cold brick wall all my life. And he only slightly warms up for her. Only her.

"Where's Juliette? Are they even home?"

"No, they went out for drinks."

"So why the fuck are you whispering?" I ask genuinely perplexed.

"I don't know."

You see? I couldn't make this shit up. She's so fucking funny.

"Let's go scaredy pants. I promise you that there are no listening devices in this foyer or anywhere in the house for that matter."

As we hop in the Rover, I realize that Elizabeth didn't follow instructions. I told her to get prettied up and while I think she's gorgeous butt naked with zero make up on; she didn't even try to dress up for me tonight.

For one, she couldn't have showered because she still has on the same tight ass gray jeans she had on this morning, but has changed into a clean white T-shirt and has on different shoes.

I'm guessing that she thinks that if she put on a tight skirt (like the one she wore for her pitch meeting) or a dress that she'd be trying too hard. That it would look very much like a date. A date she didn't want with a man who she's fooled herself into believing that she doesn't want.

I get it.

But getting people to change their minds about things they feel very strongly about is my specialty. In my line of work, I mostly use threats of bodily harm, so this time I'm going to have to be a little more creative with my strategy. Because if I'm going to be completely honest with myself about this, sometimes I have shitty ass nights of sleep, because I lie awake thinking about what I would do if some other man put his hands on Elizabeth. His mouth on her mouth. Or God forbid, his dick in her pussy.

My pussy.
That shit can never happen.
I won't let it.

First we stop at the Apple Store, and I can tell that this might be her favorite store on the planet. Some girls like Victoria's, some like Vuitton, but I can tell that my cousin loves gadgets. They turn her the fuck on.

She signs us up to see a sales tech, and we have to wait in some ridiculous queue before anyone can help us spend my money. Unbelievable. I just remembered why I never come to this store.

Some hipster looking kid, with thick black-rimmed glasses, finally comes over to us and spends the next ten minutes talking shop with Elizabeth. I don't like the way he's being so familiar with her, but I realize that one, it's probably part of his job to close the sale; and two, that even only with just a little bit of lip gloss on, Elizabeth is a stunner. So of course he would flirt with her. I shouldn't blame the dweeb.

There's no doubt about how she oozes sexiness and confidence at every given moment. She would intrigue any man. She just doesn't know it. Which is simply one more thing about her that's so attractive.

After we put in an order for eight of the latest iMac desktops, five for Philly, and the others shipped to their locations; I pull our sales tech to the side and have him ring up one of the latest laptops for me as well. I'm going to tell Elizabeth it's for Joseph, but I'm going to give it to her later tonight since she practically orgasmed after we bought all of those computers. I can't imagine what she'll do when I give her one for her own personal use. I heard her once complain that her laptop was a slow moving monster. So I think she'll like it.

After our shopping spree, I drive us away from Center City and onto the drive. I stop when we get close to Boathouse Row. My favorite place.

"Why are we stopping here?" she asks nervously.

"Remember I was taking you to do one of my favorite things?"

"Yeah?" she responds hesitantly.

A stocky, bearded man in a white windbreaker jacket approaches us with some reserve in his steps.

"Are you Mr. Masterson?" he asks as if there's no way I could be. He must be new.

"That's me."

"A pleasure to meet you. I'm Dex your captain. You can come this way. Your boat and house are ready."

Elizabeth stops me in my tracks by grasping my forearm.

"Wait a minute."

"What's wrong?"

"Are we getting on a boat? On the very deep and murky Delaware River?"

"That's right." I smile.

"But the sun is going down."

"We're going on a sunset cruise."

"A cruise boat?"

"Well it's not really the size of a cruise boat. More like a very small yacht."

"Roman—"

"You'll love it."

"This sounds like something lovers would do. This sounds like a date."

"Hell no, Elizabeth. I've done this a million times with the King brothers."

That's sort of the truth. Except every time we go boating, we are always drunk, and always fucking random club skanks on the boat. But it's probably best to leave that part of the story out.

"Really?"

"Yep. It's one of my favorite things to do. I'm not kidding."

"I wouldn't have pegged you for a sailor."

"Joseph used to take me."

We start walking to the third boathouse. I know this one well, because I've rented it before. All the boathouses are basically empty spaces available for boating groups to rent for events, but I've rented this one out and had it decorated tonight for dinner. Thanks to Jade.

"We've got at least another hour before the sun starts setting," I continue. "Let's eat first."

When we enter the boathouse there's a long, thick rectangular wooden table, which almost looks like an old door that's been restored and given a glaze top coat. The table has two place settings and is decorated with several white taper candles in silver candlestick holders as well as blue mason jars full of some sort of white flowers. They look like wild flowers of some sort; not like an arrangement I would buy a woman. I'm pleased though with how it all looks, because Jade arranged things exactly as I asked. Understated but pretty. Just like Elizabeth.

"You did this?" she asks. I like the look on her face. She seems impressed.

"Yes. I thought it'd be nice to have dinner here by the water before we go out."

"You have candlelight dinners with the King brothers when you all go boating together?"

Maybe it wasn't as understated as I thought.

"Absolutely," I lied.

But it's what she needs to hear, and I have no problem lying to get what I want.

Because I want Elizabeth.

There's no doubt in my mind about it.

14

Elizabeth

EVEN THOUGH I'M lying underneath a soft cream-colored chenille blanket, I still feel slightly chilled, as I lay on a chaise lounge on the deck of a yacht appropriately named Nauti Buoy. The sun set about an hour ago and now Roman and I are cruising under the stars and down the Delaware River. Fall is definitely coming.

Captain Dex is about to turn off the engines, so that we'll basically be buoying in the water for a while per Roman's orders. And I'm a little nervous about just floating out in such a vast body of water for a variety of reasons; but mainly because I can feel each and every movement of the water now that the engines have stopped. But I guess that's the point. To feel the motion of the river. To be lulled by it.

I take a few deep breaths to try and relax. I trust that I'm in good hands. It's just that some part of me changed after the attack. Some irrational, anxious part of me that I wish like heck would heal already. I don't trust easily anymore. Not only do I not trust many people, but I'm starting not to trust a lot of situations, especially ones that I can't control. Situations like this.

"You want a drink?" Roman turns to me and asks.

I'm not sure if the offer is coincidental, or if he knows that I'm a little on edge. Probably the latter.

"Sure. What do you have on here?"

"Everything. They make sure to stock up the bar on yachts like this."

"Okay… I'll have a glass of red anything."

"I figured that. They have a good Shiraz on board that I think you'll like. I'll get you a glass."

"Thanks."

Roman returns with a glass of wine for me and a lowball glass of whiskey for himself. He sits back down in his chaise but adjusts the back of it, so that he's completely sitting up at a ninety-degree angle. Then he reaches over and does the same for my chair.

"Let's talk."

"We have been talking." I say. "All night."

Amazingly enough we have. Roman and I have been talking about everything under the sun, and I have to admit that I'm pleasantly surprised by it. He isn't a total one-track minded sex god like I thought. I guess these are some of the "layers" that he was referring to.

Tonight we've been chatting about how to solve the national debt crisis (as if that's really possible), how to fix the domestic abuse issue in football (which seems to be the only sport he follows religiously), things I miss about my hometown, and our favorite music. I love bands in almost every genre, but after listening to dance music all night in his clubs, all Roman wants to listen to are classic rock or R&B ballads when he's relaxing at home. *Interesting.*

"Let's talk about our deal."

"What deal?" I ask trying to play dumb.

"Don't be cute, Elizabeth. The deal where you go out with me tonight, and then the other part where you call swim boy and put him out of his misery."

"I told you that I need to see him in person when I talk to him."

"I'm not sure that I agreed to that shitty arrangement."

"Do I have to start taping our conversations?" I giggle while taking another sip of my wine. He's right, it is yummy. "You agreed to it as long as I gave you that kiss we had."

"Do you really like that piece of white toast or are you just using him to make me angry?"

"I don't like what you're insinuating. Once again you think that the world revolves around you, and that I have nothing better to do than to plot and plan how I'm going to drive you crazy. I'm trying to build a life, Roman. My career. I don't want to be forty and miserable in a dead end computer job. I have dreams and plans that are way bigger than that, and trying to make you jealous isn't one of them."

"People can build a business and a relationship at the same time, Elizabeth. People do it everyday. It's not an either or situation. Or at least it doesn't have to be."

"Well, let me put it this way, if I were to ever find the time to have a social life, it would definitely be with someone like Jagger. He's sweet, good looking–"

"Boring and boring."

"Smart and respectful–"

"Plus it's a shame about that broken collarbone of his."

"What broken collarbone?" I ask alarmed.

"The one he'll get if you ever say that shit about him again to me." He grins.

"That's not funny, Roman."

"Come down below deck, I want to show you something."

"Show me what?" I ask skeptically.

"Nothing like that. I promised you I wouldn't touch you didn't I?"

He has been keeping his word. He hasn't once tried to touch my ass, my breasts, or even play with my hair.

Not once.

"All right."

We head downstairs into a sort of living room, lounge area below deck. There's long built-in fiberglass board seating along both sides of the boat, which are decorated with lots of down-filled throw pillows in variations of blue and sea green. In the middle of the built-in couches is a round polished metal table that seems to be bolted into the floor of the boat. On the table are three gift-wrapped boxes that I've never seen before.

"What are those?" I ask confused.

"These are for you."

"Whaaaat?"

"For launching your app. Just a few gifts to say congrats."

"Uh … that's really nice of you but–"

"Just open them." He waves me off. "Don't make more out of it than it is."

It doesn't take me longer than ten seconds to turn into a ten year old kid. Of course I select the biggest box to open first, because when you're a kid, bigger is always better right?

I open the first box and the first thing I see is a second soft pink colored box inside decorated with black satin ribbon. The lettering on the box reads Agent Provocateur. A store I've never heard of. Inside the pink box are layers of nicely folded black tissue paper; and wrapped inside are three exquisite lace bras with matching underwear as well as a corset and garter belt.

What's unusually pretty about all of the lingerie pieces is that they are all colored black and mustard yellow. It can't be a coincidence. He must have remembered that yellow is my favorite color. They're gorgeous.

I don't know much about fine lingerie, because I don't have the type of money to buy panties outside of Target or Walmart, but I definitely know that these are expensive. I can tell by the quality of the lace. The silk of the panties. And how the name of the brand sounds—Agent Provocateur. Exclusive. Elegant. It's pretty clear that Roman spent a lot of money. That's why internal panic alarms are already sounding off in my head by the gesture.

"Before you say anything, I think that every woman should own at least one set of matching lace underwear. A woman's body is a work of art and lingerie frames it beautifully. So please accept my gift."

I take a huge gulp of liquid courage and then respond.

"I totally get that you have a deep appreciation for the woman's body, and thank you for the gesture, but you're doing a really bad job of sticking to our no date agreement. No guy gives his friend lingerie. No man buys his cousin lingerie."

"This is not a date. I promise you. I simply remembered our conversation about how you didn't own any matching underwear and thought you might like them. End of story."

"So it's a mercy gift for the poor girl with mismatched underwear?"

"No, Elizabeth." He sighs. "It's just a gift."

He sounds like he means it, like it's the truth, yet there's something about hearing the words *just a gift* that seems unsettling. Maybe I wish he didn't mean it ... so much?

"Okay."

"Open the next one." He orders eagerly.

I open the next box and take a soft gasp. Inside is a brand new Macbook Pro. The same laptop I'm pretty sure Roman just bought for Joseph when we were at the store earlier.

"How many laptops did you buy today, Daddy Warbucks?"

"Just one."

"One? What about Joseph's?"

"Joseph would never use a new laptop unless he's absolutely forced to. I bought it for you. You were caressing it like you wanted to make love to it in the store." He chuckles. "So I thought it made sense for you to have your own, since you'll be setting up all the other computers to talk to each other. You should be able to talk to them with your own computer too right? No big deal."

No big deal?

"Well you're right about one thing. This will definitely help with the speed of the project, and I'm sure you can write it off as a business expense right?"

It makes me feel better knowing that Roman can at least write this expensive gift off. An employee expense. So it's not really a gift, because this is not really a date.

"Exactly."

"How did you get it wrapped so fast? I was with you the whole time?"

"Captain Dex wrapped it while we were on deck."

"How much did you have to pay him to do that menial task?"

He ignores that question.

"Keep unwrapping."

The third box is the smallest. It's the shape of a thin,

rectangle. Like a box you would use to gift women's gloves. I can't believe my watering eyes at what's inside.

Money ... Seventeen thousand frackin' dollars!

The exact amount stolen from me.

"Roman!"

"Listen first," he orders. "If you were a client of mine, Elizabeth, I would have tracked down all three of those douchebags, squeezed their throats for that seventeen thousand plus fucking interest, and then I would have put them in the ground, or make them at least wish they were dead. You say you really don't know what I do for a living. Well that's basically what I do.

"But since you aren't my client, and since I know that isn't your style, I'm doing the next best thing to rectify the situation. If Joseph knew about the money, he would have made you take it from him. So I'm just doing what families do. Take care of their own."

I try to speak, but he puts a finger up to silence me and continues talking.

"Now you can go do whatever the fuck it was you were going to do with the money. You're not beholden to Joseph or Juliette, your parents, or even waiting on the angel investor. You can move out of the house if you want. Or if you stay, then at least it will be on your terms. Not because you feel like you have no other options."

I am utterly speechless.

I don't know who this is sitting in front of me right now. I feel like I'm seeing a different Roman. Another layer. And it's not because of the gifts, but it's because of the thought that went behind them. The effort to make me happy. It's making me seriously consider breaking my own no date rule.

That's when I climb on top of Roman straddling his lap.

He's already hard, and it takes everything in me to not start riding his bulge right away. His hands instinctively hold me around my waist so I won't fall; and his breaths seem just as ragged as mine are shallow.

"I thought we were going to keep this Rated-G tonight, Duchess?"

"What about PG-13, Masterson?"

Roman grins.

"I should buy you shit more often if this is how you're going to react."

Our bodies start to rock in tandem with the movement of the boat. Together we feel like a lone buoy in the middle of the water.

Alone.

Erotic.

Peaceful.

Roman motions silently for me to raise my arms and then he lifts my shirt above and over my head and tosses it across the room. He slides the cups of my bra down so that my breasts are on display and my nipples pop free. As soon as the air hits them they become hard as diamonds.

Roman leans me back a bit, but makes sure to hold me so that I'm stable on his lap; he licks his lips, then clamps his mouth down on my right breast. Using just the right amount of suction, he elicits a groan from me that pleases him. I can feel him smiling with my nipple still in his mouth.

"Tell me what you want Duchess," he says with his mouth full of boob.

He knows I'm not a talker. It's like I have marbles in my mouth when it comes to dirty talk. I'm too nervous to say what I really want. I'm not sure if it's a confidence issue or just a I haven't done this before issue, but I just feel like everything I say is going to be stupid. So I don't say anything.

Roman pulls his mouth off of my breast, pops his head up, and stares me straight on with a serious look across his face.

"Tell me what you want. Do you want me?"

Do I?

"I ... think so."

"Do you think so or do you know so?"

"I know it."

"You know what I'm asking you right?"

I stay silent while Roman kneads my thighs with his strong hands and continues to speak.

"I know you want this dick right now, and I'm ready to give it to you long and deep, and for as long as you ask nicely; but I'm talking about after tonight, Duchess. Do. You. Fucking. Want. Me?"

I swallow nervously and thickly as a thin trickle of sweat rolls down my back. I feel as if my back is against the wall by the question. I guess that's why it seems as if the temperature has risen a hundred degrees in this damn boat. If I tell him yes then I'm afraid what that means moving forward. What will I tell my friends and my family? That I'm dating my cousin?

And If I tell him no? Well ... that I'm more afraid of. What if he never wants anything to do with me again? Just the thought of no Roman in my life is making me nauseous. Can I take that risk?

"I need a little more time."

"How much more?" he growls in that irresistible gravelly voice I've grown to crave like my next breath.

Before I can answer, his mouth is back on my breast. This time the left one. The sensitive one that when plea sured makes me say yes, please, and thank you to almost any frackin' thing.

"Not a lot," I say breathlessly.

Roman slides his hands inside the back of my jeans and inside my panties where he begins to massage my ass.

"I love this ass."

"I know you do." I squirm.

I can feel his thick middle finger start to travel downward and slide along the crack of my ass. My rocking starts to pick up pace as I grind against the enormous bulge in his pants. He continues to apply slight pressure to my opening with his finger as I ride him harder and harder.

This is a new sensation for me; and it's a combination of utter bliss and embarrassment. If he keeps this up much longer I'm going to come right inside my cotton panties. I never even considered that I might like someone touching me in such a private place. I pray that he doesn't want to talk about it afterwards. Roman likes that. To talk afterwards about what I liked and what I didn't like whenever we've been intimate.

"You want to come, Duchess?" he says in a way that's dripping in the promise of a long night of orgasms.

"Not yet."

"Not yet what."

"Not yet, Masterson."

"Whose ass does this belong to?" He rumbles.

I don't respond.

I just moan in frustration. I want him to stop frackin' talking. I don't want to come yet. I want to ride it out until the last possible—

Too late.

He takes his hand out of my pants and gives my ass a loud whack, and I literally start sobbing as I come. That's how spectacular that orgasm just felt.

"Masterson," I whisper reverently as I wrap my arms around his neck and lay my head on his chest.

"Yes, baby?"

"I'm afraid."

"I know, but I've got you. I will never let anything bad happen to you or to us. I just want to make you happy or at least die trying."

What does one say to that? Women wait a lifetime to hear a man say those words.

"Can you give me a little more time?"

"And then will you come to me?"

"Yes."

"Then get up and strip. Let's seal this new deal between us the right fucking way. With you riding my cock until we get back to shore."

15

Elizabeth

IT'S BEEN a little over three weeks and I haven't heard one peep from Mr. Lambert or the investment group. No one in the house has asked me about it either. Not my aunt, my uncle, or least of all Roman. They all seem to be quite content with the fact that I'm busy networking computers everyday for the betterment of the family business.

My mother hasn't asked me much either. All she's been doing lately is texting me with random tidbits about what's been going in Penn Washington. My seventh grade life science teacher Mr. Basil is dating someone that my mother knows from church, and she can't stop going on about it. My neighbor's daughter Cecilia has moved back home from college and is some sort of tax specialist with the township. Great for her Mom. Also my father recently received a pay increase from the township. The first one he's received in two years. My parents celebrated with dinner out at The Cheesecake Factory.

It's funny how she thinks sending me all these bits of trivia are going to encourage me to move back home when they are having the complete opposite effect. I want to stay as far away from all of that as I can possibly can. Which is why I'm a little anxious that I haven't heard anything from Mr. Lambert.

I've put my quest to move out of my aunt's house on hold for now. Not until I'm sure of what my plan is. Roman giving me seventeen thousand dollars has kind of put a whole new spin on things. I could technically go back to the original plan I had in place.

Hire a full time coder and live off of that money while I put my everything into School Bucks. Of course I know that money will go fast. No one can live off of seventeen thousand dollars for very long. I'd still need to find a job. Find an affordable place to live. Hire a coder from out of the country, because American freelancers cost way too much money.

Hmmm … now that I take a longer look at things, I'm not so sure that was ever really a solid plan. That's why I'm still hoping to hear good news from Mr. Lambert. More money can't hurt. It can only help my situation.

Sloan: Whatcha doing?

Me: Contemplating my life.

Sloan: No, really.

Me: About to go to work.

Sloan: Where to today?

Me: Your favorite place.

Sloan: Lotus!

Me: Yep.

Sloan: I heard it's a lot better in there now. We should party there again.

Me: Uh, really?

Sloan: Why not? We've got the family hook up to get in and you need to have some fun.

Me: Why do you always insinuate that my life is sad and boring.

Sloan: Umm well...

Me: Ha ha. Very funny. I'll let u know about Lotus later jerk.

Sloan: LOL. Later:)

I don't want to go to the club with Sloan tonight because I know for a fact that Roman will be there. There's some big event going on there tonight, which is why he wants me to double check the computers there today.

For the last three weeks, I've been able to dodge any personal scrutiny in regards to the two of us, because I've either been having my brains banged out by him in his penthouse, or we've gone out on more *non-dates* where no one knows us.

We've been out for some scrumptious dinners across town several times, we caught a show at Silk City last week, and we've been touring the city at random times via the double decker tour buses. You can hop on and hop off of them at any given time. So together we've visited the Liberty Bell for my first time, Betsy Ross's house, and Love Park.

While technically Roman is giving me some space to accept that we should be together, to go public, people that we know would know immediately that something was up if they saw us together. That's why I make myself scarce when he comes to the house to meet with Joseph, and that's why I haven't brought him around Sloan again. She thinks my "fling" with Roman is over.

Clearly I'm not ready to go public yet.

Explaining to Sloan about my feelings for Roman would probably involve a long night of drinking, screaming and insults. She would not be supportive. She would have lots of things to say about it and not good things. I'm just not in the mood for a fight tonight.

Translation ... I'm a big ass chicken.

The Lotus has transformed even more since I was last here. Since I have access to the club's computer database, I see that there are some very high profile new members of the club. Celebrities who are always in the tabloids or the gossip blogs. Many of them are athletes, and a few of them are well known entertainers.

Roman asked me the other night while I was on all fours and he was ramming into me slow, deep, and hard from behind, if I'd be his date to the club tonight. It took every ounce of will power I had to say no.

"Are you sure, Duchess?"

"Yes."

"Head down and ass up." His voice echoed in the room.

Whack!

"That's good baby. Now stay just like that while I work you just the way you like."

I whimpered a few words of gibberish, because it felt so good.

"So tell me, Duchess, are you absolutely sure you're aren't going to come with me? You want me to take someone else?"

"No." I cried.

"No what?"

"No I don't want you to take anyone else."

"So then maybe you should make sure I don't take anyone else and be my date. You can come on my dick right now like a good girl, and then you can come to the club with me tomorrow," he chuckled.

Whack!

"No." I howled.

"No? That answer doesn't make me happy, Duchess."

He stopped his deep strokes.

He stopped everything ... the bastard.

"I know." I whispered regretfully.

He pulled out and told me, *"Let's go watch Frasier in the den."*

"NOW?" I asked pitifully.

"Yep."

The orgasm bully strikes again.

That Neanderthal wouldn't let me come no matter what I tried. I tried rubbing up on him on the couch. He didn't flinch. I tried giving him a blowjob, but he just pushed me off of him and told me to "just watch the show." I even stooped to the level of saying I had to use the bathroom, so that I could take a minute and rub myself off. That's how frackin' wired he had me. But the orgasm bully was too smart for his own good, and ordered me to "go ahead and pee" after he barged inside the bathroom and bandaged some imaginary cut on his finger.

"Can't that wait until I'm finished in here?" I asked clearly frustrated that he wouldn't leave.

"I'm bleeding and you have to pee. What's more important?"

"Gah!"

So now I have the two most important people in my life wanting me to go to The Lotus with them tonight and neither one is happy with me. There's no pleasing Roman at this point. All he wants is a yes. All he ever wants is a yes from me.

But maybe I can at least salvage things with Sloan.

Me: Instead of The Lotus why don't we go somewhere a little more edgy.

Sloan: You? Edgy?

Me: Yeah I mean The Lotus is real slick and over the top now. Those aren't my type of people.

Sloan: Neither is edgy but fuck it. I'm down for whatever.

Me: Ok so you have any suggestions?

Sloan: Just wear black and I'll pick you up at nine. I'll have it all worked out by then.

Me: Thx Sloan:)

Going out with Sloan tonight is going to be pretty easy, because Roman doesn't seem to be speaking to me. I didn't hear from him at all after I left his apartment and nothing yet this morning. I almost broke down and texted him, but I refuse to give him the upper hand. That is until I stare at the laptop sitting on my dresser. My beautiful, shiny, new laptop that moves lightening fast. A gift that will always remind me of the giver, because he gave it to me to make me happy.

Me: Where are you?

Crickets.

Me: You better be in intensive care or some-thing because, otherwise I don't know why you aren't responding.

Still nothing.

One lone tear rolls down my face.

I hate this.

I hate him being mad at me.

It's not like I don't want to be with him. I do, but not at the risk of alienating every other single person in my life or his. I'm not strong like him. I mean I'm tough, but not in the same way that he is. My family can be annoying and smothering, but I love them. I don't want to lose them.

Roman seems to be able to push people away so easily. I don't know how he can sleep not knowing or caring where his mother is. As far as I know, he has zero contact with her, although I haven't once been able to convince him to talk about her for more than sixty seconds.

Baby steps I guess.

I decide to take the long way to The Lotus for no real reason except that the more Roman avoids me, the angrier I'm growing with him; so now I don't really feel much like helping him with his stupid computers. I've got my own work to do.

Since there's a very real chance that I'm not going to get the money from Mr. Lambert, I need to figure out some alternative ways to get the money. I need to fund my business. Not take care of his.

Since I'm later than I intended, there are several staff people who have already arrived at The Lotus and are setting up for what looks like some sort of performance tonight.

"Hey, Elizabeth." I'm greeted at the door.

"Hey, Jarrett." Jarrett is The Lotus's new manager. Larry has been made a weekend manager, and Marco is still the bar manager.

"Office is open; go on inside."

"Getting ready I see."

"Yeah it should be a fun night."

"What's going on tonight again?"

"Surprise performance. It's going to be an acoustic set by Maroon 5"

"Wow!"

Jarrett cocks his head to the side.

"You didn't know?"

"Uh, no."

"It's going to be a real sexy event. Lots of celebrities will be here. I'm surprised your cousin didn't tell you."

"I'm sure he meant to." I lie. "I've just been so swamped with work, I probably didn't give him much of an opportunity to tell me."

"Sure. Well I've got to go check on the sound people, so help yourself to the office. Holler if you need anything."

"Thanks Jarrett."

After about twenty minutes running the computer's new database software through it's paces, I pop my head up after hearing the door lock click.

It's him.

"Elizabeth."

"Asshole," I greet Roman in return.

Except I don't really mean it. My anger dissipated the moment he walked through the threshold. Roman looks absolutely, without a doubt, hot. He's wearing his usual go to uniform of a worn tee, snug jeans, boots and a custom blazer. His five o'clock shadow is heavy and his head freshly shorn. And those eyes…

"You're here late," he comments.

"I'll be finished in about ten more minutes."

"Then you're leaving?"

"Sure am."

"What's wrong with you?"

"Nothing."

"Stop lying."

"Did you get a text from me today?"

"Yeah."

"Yeah?! Why didn't you respond?"

"I was tied up."

The first image that pops into my head when he says this is that he has been tied up all day banging some other woman. A woman with long legs and fake breasts. A type of woman who's never heard of the national debt and who only knows football players based on the salaries they make or the celebrities they've screwed. A type of woman that would jump at the chance to shout off of the rooftop that she was with Roman. A woman who he's conveniently not

related to. So basically a woman that is the complete opposite of me.

"What's with all the black?"

He probably is asking me about my outfit, because it's
so clearly obvious that I'm either about to go clubbing or
about to rob a bank. I never wear all black; but tonight I
have on a black tank top, tight black skinny jeans with a
gold skinny belt, my favorite black pumps, and probably
entirely too much make up.

"I have plans."

"Is that right."

"Yep."

Roman walks slowly up to and around the desk I'm
sitting at. I can smell him. He's been drinking already
tonight. Cognac I think. He pops a few M&M's in his
mouth and sits on the edge of the desk directly in front
of me.

"Where are you going without me, Duchess?"

"Just out." I bend my head down. I can't face him. I
feel extraordinarily guilty that I won't be here with him
tonight, and I'm pretending as if I'm the one mad
at him.

"If I told you not to go would you listen?"

"Probably not."

"And there lies the problem doesn't it."

I don't think he's waiting for an actual response to that
statement, so I stay silent.

"You don't listen to a fucking thing I say. You do whatever you want. Well I'm going to give you what you want
then—"

"Wait." I anxiously interrupt. This doesn't sound good.

"I'm done."

"What do you mean done?"

"You know what the fuck I mean."

"Why!? Because I won't come to your stupid show tonight?"

Crap I didn't mean for that to come out the way it did.

"Because this is dumb!" he roars. "Because I don't beg for pussy, and I'm not going to start now. Not even from you."

"So I'm just that to you now?!"

"You know you're not *just* that. You're every fucking thing. But I can't seem to make you see that. So if you don't see it, if you don't feel it, if you don't want it, then I'm just the fuck done."

"I thought you were going to give me some more time. I thought you were going to wait for me!"

I feel a heavy sensation on my chest.

I think it's panic.

"Your time is up." He says coldly.

And now I'm pretty sure that the tears are coming next, but I'll do almost anything to make sure that he doesn't see them.

This is my out.

Right here.

This moment.

He's serving it to me on a silver platter, and I need to take it before I destroy us both.

"Then let me finish up in here, and I'll be on my way."

I bow my head lower as a tear drops on the keyboard in front of me, but Roman either doesn't see or doesn't care and the next thing I know, the only sounds I hear are Roman's heavy booted footsteps walking away from me and the office door slamming shut.

16

Roman

"SHIT LOOKS GOOD IN HERE, ROME."

My crew is all here. Good thing too, because I'm ten seconds away from getting good and fucking drunk.

Cutter is complimenting me on the new custom love seats I ordered for the VIP area, Camden is checking on a couple of things in the back for the performance seating, and Jade is flirting with Mr. Rico fucking Suave himself— the bar manager Marco. Why I still employ him is beyond me.

The King brothers and I came up with the idea of hosting live concerts in The Lotus to justify our exclusive membership price of seventy-five hundred for the year, as well as to attract more high profile clientele. We want the celebrities we have in our pockets, like Mendez, to get a few pictures canoodling with other celebrities in an approved setting. A setting that we control. No drugs. No driving home drunk. Basically they're paying us twice. Once to party and then again to keep them out of trouble.

It's a brilliant plan that Joseph actually masterminded.

Instead of resenting him so much, I'm starting to think it would be a smarter idea for me to learn as much as I can from him. He may not be the best father on the planet, but he's certainly an expert on how to turn ten dollars into ten thousand. And that's a legacy that a whole lot of sons would love to have passed down to them from their fathers.

"Yeah it does," I agree with Cutter on the new decor. "The munchkin had a lot to do with it." I say giving Jade her props.

"You should have set up a back room though. Like a champagne room. I like my pussy fresh and hot off the dance floor."

"You really need a back room for that? I'm sure you can find a corner somewhere in here." I joke.

"I'm not seventeen anymore, Rome. I stopped fucking in club corners a long ass time ago." Cutter chuckles. "So what's up with the guest list? Did you invite those models from New York? What was the blonde's name? Amy? Amelia?"

"I don't know. Jade handled all of that. I'm sure they're coming."

Cutter raises his eyebrows.

"You love model pussy. So what's up?"

"Nothing."

"You're lying, which is something you never do, so it must be serious. Therefore I'll leave your moody ass alone. Just fix your face by tonight. You look scarier than usual, and I don't want you scaring away my model pussy." He laughs.

"Shut up asshole."

The night couldn't be going any better than it is. That little prick Marco did something right for once and made sure to hire a few new girls that drunk ass business men like to throw money at. High tits, tight asses, flat stomachs and somewhat slutty. Perfect. They've got men buying bottles in here left and right and the bar is probably going to have its best night yet.

The set is still going on downstairs while I'm up here sitting in the VIP area with my good friend Jack Daniels. Contemplating what woman will get the fine privilege of breaking me from my Elizabeth fast. I'm not eating that pussy ever again. The problem though is that I can't make a decision. Maybe I drank too much already. Maybe I'm just tired from all the running I was doing today. I don't know what the fuck is going on, but not one of these bitches is making my dick hard.

"Hey, boss man."

Speaking of not making my dick hard– it's Jade.

"What's up, little nugget?"

"I really don't want to tell you this."

"So why are you? Go find some rich guy's head to play with downstairs."

"You'll fire me if I don't tell you."

"What now, Jade?"

"I've been keeping an eye on that kid like you asked me to."

Suddenly my hackles rise. I'm not going to like this shit. "And?"

"Elizabeth's boy is definitely back in town."

"Don't call him that," I say through gritted teeth. "Has he called her yet?"

Is that what the fuck she's doing right now instead of being here with me?

"I don't think so, but I put an eagle eye on his new place, and my guy just texted me a pic. Take a look."

Jade scrolls down and enlarges a picture on her phone of a small apartment. The living room area. There isn't much to it. It's definitely a guy's place. A sofa, two chairs, a fireplace, a flat screen and a small side table, but it's the decorations that are a kick to my gut.

A picture of a smiling Elizabeth on the mantle of the fireplace.

Two pictures of Elizabeth and the dickhead together on the small table.

Some sort of college newspaper clipping that features Elizabeth, fucking framed, and hung on that douchebag's wall over top of the sofa.

"This fucker is insane!" I bellow.

"Okay, calm down, I agree. He may be off a little. I mean it isn't exactly a shrine, but he's definitely having some sort of a break with reality. Either that or maybe she's still—"

"Shut it, Jade."

"Well it's possible. I mean don't act like it's not a possibility. Without actually tapping her cell phone and shit, we don't know who she's been talking to. She could be encouraging his ass for all—"

"I know she isn't." I cut her off.

"Really? Well where is your precious Elizabeth right now? Do you know that? She sure as shit isn't here."

"She's out."

"With the little NBA brat no doubt. Into all sorts of trouble with that one."

"Probably." I take another swig of my Jack.

It's the only thing that can comfort me now, because I really want to hurt this Ethan kid, and it doesn't even matter that he hasn't done anything lately. Just the fact that he's breathing the same air as Elizabeth has my trigger finger itchy like a motherfucker.

Fuck it.

I need to find her.

I should have put a tail on all four of them myself.

Elizabeth, Ethan, Jagger and Sloan.

That way I would have complete control over this situation. I have never been this sloppy before in my life. If this were a client I was working, I would know everything, down to what type of toilet paper each of them fucking buys.

Once again I'm flying blind. I need to remember this night and make sure that I never fucking repeat it. Family or not. Girl I'm trying to impress the fuck out of or not. This sloppy shit is not me. So since I'm blind, I'm going to have to rely on my instincts. Which are good but never a sure thing.

I know girls like Sloan. I've fucked a hundred of them. They're beautiful, spoiled, and entitled. Some are social climbers, some are thrill chasers, but Sloan is a fun seeker. She just wants to party and bullshit her way through life. There are a lot of places in the city to do just that tonight, but only a few where all-black, casual attire is acceptable.

Elizabeth has to be in one of them.

Lucky for me, third time is the charm. I can spot that spectacular ass shaking a mile away.

"Hey, Roman." A loud, feminine voice distracts me momentarily from my mission.

"Hey," I respond not paying much attention to who I'm talking to, because I'm busy watching the asshole that's dancing with Elizabeth. He's enjoying it way too fucking much.

"It's Patricia," she says a bit indignantly. I guess I'm supposed to remember her.

"What's up, Patricia?"

"You want to dance?"

"I don't dance."

"But you move so well in other places, I'm sure you can dance just as good too."

Patricia gives me a drunk, flirty smile, but it does nothing to ring any bells for me. I don't remember this chick. I'd probably need to see her with her clothes off from the neck down to have any recollection. And even then my memory would probably be sketchy.

"Listen, darlin', I've got to handle some business right now. So you go on and ask somebody else all right?"

"Awww, don't be like that, *Romeo*," she unattractively slurs.

Then tipsy Patricia slides her sweaty palm down my face, and I quickly swat it away like the little annoying gnat that she is. But it only takes that split second for me to lose Elizabeth in the crowd.

FUCK!

I start walking through the sea of bodies that are writhing to some god awful Little Wayne song and miraculously I spot the glamazon. She's flirting with some nondescript dude, so I walk up on them to get some answers.

"Glamazon."

She rolls her eyes immediately upon meeting mine.

"What the hell are you doing here?"

"Looking for my cousin."

"Why? She's out with me."

I give nondescript dude one hard grit, he sizes me up, then walks his ass away.

"I need to talk to her."

"Oh my God, you scared my date away. Don't you have like a hundred clubs to run or men to pistol-whip? Why the hell are you bothering us?"

What has Elizabeth been telling this bitch?

"I'm going to pretend that you didn't just say some very offensive shit to me and ask you again where the fuck my cousin is."

"How should I know? Dancing no doubt. We are in a club."

Once again I try to understand why Elizabeth hangs out with her. Women are supposed to stick together in a club. Especially a grimy one like this. Any fucking thing could happen.

"Why are you such a bitch?"

"Because you are such an asshole. Every time Elizabeth talks about you she has nothing good to say. You need to stop fucking with her head."

"Whatever. Has Elizabeth mentioned anything about Ethan to you lately?"

"Why?"

She doesn't look the least surprised by my question. She knows something. I could threaten her, but that wouldn't be polite, and Elizabeth would probably never speak to me again. So since I can't have that, maybe I've got to handle this another way.

Be nice, Roman.

"Elizabeth and I may argue, but she's family, and her parents would kill me if anything happened to her on my watch. Ethan put her in harms way, and it wasn't that damn long ago that he did it. He's a drug addict and he's dangerous. I'm just trying to keep her safe."

I see a slight change in Sloan's facial expression.

"You think he's dangerous?"

Her eyes shift.

"Has she talked to him, Sloan?"

"Well no, but he called me."

"You?"

"He didn't call Bitsy, because she asked him not to contact her anymore when you guys were in the Bahamas, so he called me."

"When?"

"A couple of times. The last time I talked to him was earlier today."

Today! I just want to smack some common sense into this little glamazon's head, but I can see that I'm dealing with a girl with a lot of mouth but limited street smarts. She can't smell one bit of trouble, just like Elizabeth can't. She's all talk.

"Tell me everything he said."

Turns out that Ethan has been working Sloan for information about Elizabeth for at least two weeks. Asking her about her new job (with me). Asking her if she plans on moving out of my father's house. Pleading his sorry ass case. Telling Sloan that he loves Elizabeth. That he just wants another chance to show her that, and some other bullshit about his swimming career, blah, blah, blah. Whatever the fuck.

"I need you to listen to me carefully, Sloan. Don't tell Elizabeth I was here. It'll just make her angry. But when Ethan calls you again, I need you to arrange a time to meet him and then tell me where."

"That's a pretty tall order. Lie to my best friend. Set up another friend. You're not going to hurt him are you?"

"Will you do this or not?"

"If I don't do it what are you going to do?"

"Handle shit without you."

"All right, all right. It's very possible that he could end up here tonight."

"Why!?"

"I told him we were coming here. I thought it would be an easier way for them to see each other again without a lot of drama. You know in a public place."

My eyes start to immediately scan the room. I'm looking for dickhead or Elizabeth, or God forbid the both of them together.

After about the longest five minutes of my life, I see a massive mop of dark, curly hair. I would know that head of hair anywhere. It's been threaded through my fingers many fucking nights. I've yanked that hair back as I pounded its owner from behind. I've sniffed that hair, curled it between my fingers, and even brushed it in the mornings.

I've found her and now that I have, I want her ass more than ever.

"Duchess." I say to myself almost in relief.

She whips her head around while the man she's talking to still has his hands wrapped around her hips. I can't believe my fucking eyes.

It's him.

"Roman," Elizabeth says while reaching for my arm. I can tell by the glint in her eyes that she's happy as fuck to see me. It feels almost as good to see that look on her face as it does when she's coming apart for me; but my brain can't compute all these conflicting visuals.

Elizabeth happy to see me.

Ethan with his hands on her.

Elizabeth reaching for me.

Elizabeth actually talking to this asshole.

"You've got three fucking seconds to take your hands

off her ass, or I swear to motherfucking God that I'll snap that little scrawny swimmer's neck of yours."

"You should see someone about this unhealthy fixation you have for your cousin."

WHAT! All of a sudden this dickwad had the nerve to grow some balls?

I'm about to crack his jaw wide open when Elizabeth walks directly up on me and cradles my face with her hands.

"I'm sorry, Masterson."

Fuck she's fighting dirty.

"I told him to stay the fuck away, Elizabeth."

"I know you did, but it's just a coincidence that we are both at the same club. It's a smaller world than you think. We were bound to run into each other."

Is she lying right now or does she really believe that ridiculous shit?

"Elizabeth, he planned this shit!"

Doesn't she see that?

"It doesn't matter."

"His hands were all over your ass!"

"My therapist is on speed dial if you want to talk to some one, bro," the little fucker says.

"Say one more fucking word. Pretty please. I double dare you." I taunt him while clenching my right fist.

I can tell he wants to tell me to fuck off. Badly. He wants to show off in front of Elizabeth, and stand up to me to prove some meaningless point to her.

"Ethan," she warns him. "Just go."

I'm still wound tight like a highly strung guitar chord. Ready to pop at a moment's notice as Ethan walks away from the two of us. His peripheral vision still on me as he moves through the bodies on the dance floor towards the exit. I'm just waiting for one slip up. One sign to let me know that I'm not being totally irrational; that this mother-fucker is testing my resolve.

I get it just when he thinks he's out of Elizabeth's range of sight.

The little prick winks at me.

Elizabeth

ROMAN HAS PUT me on a Masterson-style punishment for the last 24 glorious hours. I told Aunt Juliette that I was staying over Sloan's for a girl's weekend, but instead I am in the Masterson Penthouse Suite getting orgasm bullied room by room by room.

Yesterday it was his bedroom. Today it's the living room.

"Strip and go stand in front of that mirror."

Roman owns a massive floor length, distressed wood framed mirror that he keeps propped up against a wall in his living room. After I take off the last of my clothes, I stand there and stare at myself waiting for his next instruction.

It doesn't come right away. Instead there is a pocket of tense silence between us. Him staring at me while I stare at myself. And immediately all of my insecurities start to pop up, and I look down and away from the mirror. My hips seem to be growing in width the longer I gawk at myself.

"Head up," his heavy voice commands.

After another very long minute or so, Roman walks up

behind me. He's fully clothed and I'm butt naked. His arms snake around my waist and then he takes several fingers and slides them gently between my folds. It's instinctive for me to close my eyes when he does something that feels so delicious, but he wants them open.

"Open up," he says. "Open up everything to me Duchess. Your eyes. Your legs. Even this." He taps my chest where my heart is.

He's staring intently at me while he stands behind me in the mirror.

"Why do you want me?" I ask.

It's probably the most raw, the most honest thing I've ever asked him or anyone. Because for the life of me, I don't understand why the hell Roman wants me and all the inevitable baggage that will come from being with me.

"Look at you."

His fingers start to rub a little deeper. My breathing starts to become shallow as he uses his other hand to hold me under my left breast. He uses his thumb to gently rub back and forth across my nipple and the mixture of watching what he's doing to me in the mirror and the sensations of how it all feels is about to quickly make me come undone.

"You're so fucking pretty Duchess. Especially when you look like this. Flushed, sweaty, spread wide and wet for me. Why wouldn't I want you? Why wouldn't any man fight for this?"

I lean over and support myself with my palms flat on the mirror after that comment. I'm so wet that his fingers are easily slipping and sliding inside of me. Even though I've been with him many times, I'm still a little embarrassed by my body's reaction. How can I be this wet and he isn't even inside me yet? Is this normal?

"Tell the truth, Duchess. You only get this wet for me right?"

It's like he's in my head.

"Yes, Masterson."

"What do I have to do to get you this wet all the time for me?"

"Exist," I mutter.

I love the heavy rumble of his laugh. It rolls and echoes around the room and inside my belly. I could listen to it all day, everyday.

"That's all I have to do, baby? Is just exist?"

"Everything you do makes me wet, Masterson."

"That's a good answer, Duchess. You're learning. That's why you're so fucking smart. Too smart sometimes. Maybe you think some things over a little too much, analyzing things to death, when you just need to feel."

"What do you mean?" I pant.

"Where's your favorite place to sit in my house?"

"The chaise."

He stops touching me and orders me to, "Go lie on it."

Roman goes inside his bedroom and comes back out with a small dark blue duffle bag. He unzips it and pulls out a small plastic package. Inside is a brand new bullet vibrator. I know very well what they look like because I own one. Although this one doesn't have a controller attached. It seems to be wireless. Just a small silver, egg-shaped vibrator. Why am I not surprised that the orgasm bully owns his own toy bag.

"Raise your arms above your head and clasp them on top of the chaise."

I do as I'm told. Experience tells me that these scenes a.k.a. punishments are always better for me if I follow instructions and keep my mouth shut. Of course that's not always possible.

"Spread your legs and keep your feet flat on either side of the chaise. Excellent. Now you know what to do next right?"

I nod my head in understanding.

"What comes next, Masterson?" I ask.

"This is a lesson all about letting go and just feeling shit. So next I'm going to slide this vibrator inside your pussy."

I gulp for a minute in shock.

"Then what, Masterson?"

"Then I'm going to suck on your clit for no less than thirty minutes."

I clench the entire time he describes what he's going to do me. I could come right the hell now. I'm never going to make it for a half an hour much less five minutes.

I'm in big frackin' trouble.

"You remember the rules right?"

"All my orgasms belong to you."

"That's right, baby. That means you don't come until I say you do. That's my only rule. If you come without permission, we start all over. Got it?" He grins when he asks me that.

He knows I'm going to fail. He's counting on it.

The vibrator is cool and smooth as Roman easily works it inside of my drenched walls. I immediately clamp down on it as it goes in, and I have to take a few deep calming breaths to bring myself down. It's not even buzzing yet, but Roman has me so damn excited that just the sensation of something going inside of me is making my vagina very happy.

He digs back into his bag and pulls out the part I must have missed– the controller. It looks like the sort of contraption you would see someone use with a remote controlled car, and evidently it works exactly the same.

When he turns the knob slightly to the right, I begin to hear a muffled buzzing sound vibrating inside of me.

My eyes roll inside the back of my head.

"Eyes on me, Duchess."

Shit.

"Okay."

"Watch me."

"Okay," I pant.

Still fully dressed, Roman faces me and straddles the chaise. Then he bends down and begins to kiss the insides of my thighs. He hasn't even made it to my clit yet, and I'm ready to scream bloody murder.

"FRACK!" I scream.

When I do, Roman turns the vibrator up a little faster to further raise the intensity of my orgasm. I scream again, but the words are garbled and incoherent since Roman is sliding his tongue in my mouth to swallow them. When my breathing starts to slow a bit, Roman turns the vibrator all the way off and lifts his head to speak.

"You fucked up, Duchess."

I can't respond. I'm too winded and dazed.

"Maybe you aren't the fast learner that I thought you were. The rules were simple and clear. The test was easy, but you failed. Now we're going to have to try it all over again."

"I can't–"

"You can and you will. What's your favorite ice cream flavor?"

"Chocolate."

"You're in luck," he grins sinisterly. "I've got some chocolate here. Stay where you are. Don't move."

Much of Roman's penthouse is really one big large open space, so I can see everything that he's doing in the kitchen from the living room. He's wetting a paper towel with warm water. Then he's scooping some chocolate fudge ice cream in a small white ceramic bowl. And now he's walking back over to me.

He wipes between my legs with the warm paper towel but keeps the vibrator inside me. Next he feeds me a scoop of chocolate ice cream, then himself, and right afterwards starts sucking on my clit.

The sensation is amazing because my body is on fire, but his mouth is frigid from eating the ice cream. It feels so erotic yet soothing. As he continues expertly eating me out, he turns the knob of the controller to damn near number eight on the dial and my back immediately arches. Then just as quickly he turns the vibrator down and off and now I'm coming quickly down.

Over the next fifteen minutes Roman continues eating ice cream, eating me, and turning the vibrator up then down. By the last time he turns it up, I can't hold on any longer, and my orgasm is so powerful that I feel the adrenaline rush to my head like a freight train.

It renders me frackin' speechless, and I begin to tear up.

"You know that tears don't move me, Duchess. Not even yours. You fucked up again. So we're going to have to start this shit all over again."

"What's the lesson I'm suppose to be learning again?" I challenge.

"That nobody touches what's mine, and you let that asshole Ethan put his hands on my hips and my ass. They belong to me."

"Right … okay I think I've learned my lesson, Roman."

"What the fuck did you just say?"

"I meant Masterson. I've learned my lesson, Masterson."

"No," he shakes his head. "I don't really think you did."

Oh. God.

"This time I want you to get up."

"Are you going to take this thing out?"

"Nope."

I'm moving a little slower than normally, because I've just had two earth shattering orgasms, and I have a vibrator stuck up my hoo hah; but I still manage to stand up. Roman gives me a light peck on the lips and then lies down on the chaise watching me. I'm anxiously awaiting what comes next. So I ask him the required question.

"What are you going to do next, Masterson?"

"Well *you* are going to go in the kitchen and get me a glass of water. I've been working hard eating that pussy. I need a cool drink."

I clench my eyes shut for a moment and gather my resolve. Fine. He wants water. I'll get it and throw it in his face. He's just being plain ole' mean at this point.

I take several steps, allowing myself to become adjusted to the foreign object inside of me when I hear and then feel the familiar buzz inside of me again.

Dammit!

I stop in my tracks and then so does the vibrator.

When I start walking again, he turns the vibrator up again.

He continues this torturous game of starting and stopping his little toy until I reach the island in the kitchen and lean on it for dear life.

My breathing is very heavy now. My legs quivering.

I want to come.

I want him inside of me.

I want to kill him.

I wonder what he'll do if I throw this damn fruit bowl at his head.

I turn my head to glower at him, and I catch Roman

staring at me with those smoldering coal eyes. I know that he wants to get inside of me in the worst way, but he thinks he's proving some point by punishing us both with this orgasm bully game of his. I can't wait to get this frackin' glass of water! I swear it's going right in his face.

After a few deep breaths I continue on my journey to the cabinet for a glass. Then to the water dispenser on his fridge.

"I want ice," he calls out in the most cavalier manner.

I mutter the word jackass under my breath, but not quietly enough, because he hears me and turns the vibrator up on what I think is speed nine or ten.

My knees start to buckle, so I grab onto the edge of the kitchen sink.

Then he turns it off.

"Don't be a smart ass, Duchess. Just get the water and bring it here."

"Shut up, Masterson!" I yell with tears streaming down my face.

Even at my expense, the rumble of his laughter warms me from the inside out. I love it. I think I love almost everything about his sadistic ass. That's my damn problem.

"Come on, baby. Bring me the water," he says in a soothing tone that I've learned over time not to trust one single bit.

I fill the tall glass with crushed ice and then water. I fill it only three quarters of the way in case he turns this thing back on, on my way back. That way I won't spill any if I have to suddenly stop. I start walking very slowly back across the living room and surprisingly Roman doesn't turn the vibrator back on. Thank goodness. I think he knows that if he did, I'd come immediately, and I'm pretty sure that defeats the purpose at this point in his little game.

I know that I said I was going to toss the water in his

face, and I seriously considered it for three seconds, but I'm not a moron. I know that there'd be hell to pay if I did that. And not in the sexy, playful Masterson way— but probably in the mean, nasty Roman way.

"Thanks, Duchess."

"You're welcome," I say a little sarcastically.

He smirks at me while he takes the glass and throws back the entirety of it in two long gulps. Then he gingerly licks a droplet off of his top lip when he's done, and in the moment I start to fantasize just where that tongue really belongs. He's so damn sexy it's criminal.

Then Roman swings his legs to the side of the chaise and starts to silently undress. First his boots. Which he unlaces and places neatly by the wall very slowly and precisely. Then he pulls his T-shirt off, revealing the body ink I love to trace with my fingertips every time we're together. Next he stands up with his back to me and drops his pants to the floor in one smooth move. When he turns around I can't help but be immediately drawn to the large erection bulging through his black boxers.

We lock eyes and in that moment, he slides his boxers to the floor and steps out of them. Then he lies back down on the chaise with his arms bent and hands clasped behind his head.

"Come sit on my face, Duchess."

I'm hesitant at first because I'm not sure how steady I can remain straddling Roman across this chair, but he holds onto my hips and ass while I mount up and makes sure I'm stable before he reaches on the side of the chaise and turns the knob of that dreaded controller.

This time he only turns it to just a slow buzz. Not enough to send me straight to the moon, but just enough to annoy the frack out of me ... until it doesn't. It starts to feel really good after a minute or so, and that's when I place my palms flat on the wall above his head to stabilize myself, because I know what's coming next.

His mouth.

It doesn't take long for me to explode.

Roman is precise and thorough when he uses that dirty mouth of his.

My breathing is quick and labored now. My body is hot and sticky. I see flashes of blinding white light and am probably speaking in tongues as Roman reaches inside me and pulls out the vibrator. He tosses it on the side of the chaise for the time being and quickly rolls on a condom, then lifts me to position me directly above his jutting cock.

As I slide myself down, the feeling is absolute bliss, and it's in this moment that I know for sure that I'm where I belong.

So we stay like that for the next twelve hours.

Elizabeth

WHEN I RETURN BACK HOME from Roman's for the weekend, I feel like a teenaged girl who's covering up a hicky from their parents and can't look them straight in the eyes.

"Is everything all right Elizabeth?" my aunt asks with concern etched across her face.

"Yes, Auntie, I'm just tired from hanging out with Sloan all weekend."

"You guys went out I take it?"

"Well ... we stayed up late."

"It's been so long since I had a girls night out, I forgot what they were like. How's the job going?"

"It's fine."

"Roman isn't riding you too hard is he?"

The irony of that statement is incredible.

"No, Auntie. He pretty much lets me do all the work."

"Ah, that's good. I thought he was going to be a problem for a minute."

"Nope."

"Good then. I'm roasting two rosemary chickens

tonight, and thought I'd invite him to come for dinner. As long as you two are getting along, it shouldn't be a problem right?"

"I didn't say we liked each other."

Dinner tonight is not a good idea. Especially when I can literally still smell Roman all over me.

Juliette chuckles. "Well you don't hate each other either."

"No."

"Well then we can have a family dinner."

Sigh.

"Sure, ok. I look forward to it."

"Excellent!"

Exit stage right. Texting Roman now.

Me: Juliette is going to ask you to come for dinner. Say no.

Roman: Hi baby.

Me: Grrr! Hi. Did you hear me?

Roman: I miss you too.

Me: ROMAN!

Roman: What's she cooking?

Me: Why?

Roman: Because I want to know.

Me: Rosemary chicken.

Roman: Oh hell no! I'm coming.

Me: Don't tell me. That's your favorite meal too.

Roman: Hell yes.

Me: You like everything she cooks.

Roman: If you cook for me I won't have to eat her cooking.

Me: I don't cook.

Roman: Well you better learn because as you can see I like to eat:)

Me: Obviously:)
Roman: You have a dirty mind, Duchess.
Me: And you're just dirty period.
Roman: You love it.
Me: So are you coming or not?
Roman: What do you think?
Me: Can you call me right now plz?
My cell phone rings immediately.

"Hello?"

"What'd you want to tell me?"

"Think about what I'm saying, Roman. They're going to figure it out if you come over here."

"No they won't. I'll be on my best behavior."

"Didn't you say Joseph was super smart and can sniff that sort of thing out?"

"I got this, Duchess."

"You're sure?"

"Absolutely."

"All right then I'll see you later."

"Wear a dress."

"I thought you said you were going to behave!"

"Only if you wear a dress."

"All right, Roman, but I swear—"

"I know, I know. I'll see you tonight."

"All right bye."

Juliette's chicken smells heavenly. Maybe it's because I've been on the computer all day and forgot to eat, or maybe it's because she actually missed her calling and should have been a chef. I can tell by the variety of savory scents wafting upstairs and the fact that the sun is going down that dinner is very much ready.

I jump in the shower for all of five minutes, just long enough to rub body wash over my entire body and do a quick rinse, then I lotion and throw on one of my favorite floral dresses with Roman's mustard and black lingerie underneath minus the garters.

I know. I'm just asking for trouble.

The flower print of the dress isn't too overwhelming, just a soft yellow rose print, on a cap-sleeved black dress that hits my legs right above the knee. I brush my hair back in a messy bun and apply a pale pink lip gloss. I think I look clean and attractive, but not like I've tried too hard.

"You need any help, Auntie?" I ask in an unusually chipper voice.

Oh crap. I've got to tone it down. I'm so worried about how Roman's going to behave when it's me that's most likely the weak link.

"Oh I love that dress, Elizabeth."

"Thanks. It's old but really comfortable."

"Oh really? You wouldn't know it was old. It's pretty and it's perfect for you. Well, let's see. I'm pretty much done here. The chicken is finished. I roasted some root vegetables with it. I stuffed it because Joseph likes stuffing. I also made a side of roasted brussel sprouts too and of course I picked up some fresh sourdough bread from the Smith Bakery."

"That all sounds really good. I'm starving too."

"I figured you were. You haven't been in the kitchen all day. How's your website thing going?"

"It's an app, Auntie."

"Oh right an app."

"Things will be better soon. I'm going to hire a coder soon who's going to help me work out the kinks."

With the seventeen thousand dollars Roman gave me.

"Oh that's great, and if things don't work out with that

investor you pitched, you know you can always ask your uncle for the money. He would love to invest in your business."

"I know he would, but I'd rather keep trying to get funding on my own."

"Of course sweetie. That makes perfect sense."

The doorbell rings.

"Oh that must be your cousin. Get the door honey. I swear I don't understand why that boy won't use his key."

When I open the door all I see is over six feet of pure hotness staring down at me like I'm a hot fudge brownie sundae or something else really good to eat.

"Good evening, Miss Hill." He grins.

"Good evening." I try to hide my grin with a covered hand. "Your stepmother wants to know why you never use your key."

"Not my house." He says as he walks through the threshold brushing slightly by me. A few of his fingers lightly touching my thigh when he goes by.

"Roman." I hear the calm and deep voice of my uncle acknowledging Roman's presence.

"Joseph."

"After we eat I have to talk to you about some business, since you haven't been by here in a while."

"Yep."

Dinner is amazing.

Juliette has set the table beautifully complete with cloth napkins and fall themed serving platters. Both Roman and I remain quiet throughout dinner though, and barely interact with each other except for the one time he went for a quick feel of my thigh under the table. It's a miracle I didn't jump clear through the ceiling. The night had been so quiet and uneventful that I wasn't expecting it. He caught me totally off guard, just like he likes it.

"So how's the network coming, Elizabeth?" Joseph asks me while taking a small bite of chicken. If I didn't know any better, I'd swear that my uncle is completely on to us.

"I'm basically finished." I say.

"Well not quite," Roman adds.

"No ... I'm pretty sure I would know if I'm finished and I am."

"So when will you be completely finished?" Joseph asks.

"I can finish up everything I need to do from here in about two days. I just need to run a check and make sure the network is talking to each other nicely. It was a little difficult walking the techs in Miami and New York through what I needed them to do. So I definitely want to check in with them again."

"Maybe you should run by the clubs and handle it yourself directly," Joseph suggests.

"Run by them?"

"Drive up to New York and fly down to Miami. Shouldn't take you long."

"Umm, I'm not sure—" I say hesitantly.

"Have you paid her yet, Roman?" My uncle asks.

"We're still working that part out."

Joseph wipes his mouth with his napkin and places it and his fork both down on the table. He gives Roman a hard stare then turns his attention back to me.

"What does a job of this magnitude usually cost, Elizabeth? What would you charge if you didn't know us?"

"That's the thing, Uncle Joseph, I'm staying in your house for free. I'm fine with you paying me whatever you think is fair. I was happy to do it."

"So why exactly haven't you paid her?" He basically ignores me and directs the question to Roman.

"Joseph," Aunt Juliette warns. "Not right now."

"I'm confused as to who is running this shit with all this

backseat fucking management you're doing. Is it me or you? Until we're clear about that, I don't know who should be paying her."

"What did I tell you about raising your voice in my house."

"Maybe you two should have that talk now," my aunt interrupts. "Elizabeth, can you help me clear the dishes?"

I'm not sure what is happening right now, but I don't like it. I especially don't like that I have something to do with it.

Roman and Joseph stare silently at each other for what seems like forever. Almost like two strong bulls sizing each other up before they meet in the center of the ring.

I'm afraid. Not for myself or anything like that, but because I've seen glimpses of Roman's love for his father during our times together. I know that he yearns for Joseph's respect and approval, even if he doesn't realize it himself.

"What is the deal with those two?" I ask as I scrape plates.

"The deal that has always been between fathers and sons I suppose. With a little bit of Mom issues on the side."

"Roman doesn't talk about his mom at all. Where is she?"

Aunt Juliette raises a brow at me.

"Why would he talk about his mother with you? I thought you two barely spoke at all."

"Like I said, we don't hate each other. We speak from time to time." I pray that she bought that.

"His mother is responsible for a lot of frightening and painful times in Roman's childhood. I don't think he'll ever forgive Joseph for not being there more to help him, or to maybe save his mother from herself."

"Is she ... dead?"

"We don't think so, but we don't know for sure."

"With all of your money and resources, no one has been able to find her?"

"I guess not." Aunt Juliette clams up. "Can you pour me a small glass of wine honey?"

"Sure."

"The bottle is still out on the buffet table."

"Okay."

When I peek back out into the dining room to get the bottle of chardonnay we were drinking with dinner, I see that both Roman and Joseph are gone. They must have gone into the office to talk. I just hope they aren't verbally tearing each other to shreds in there. They both have extremely acerbic tongues when pushed.

I'm not sure how long I stand in the dining room, waiting to see if I can hear any yelling or God forbid punches being thrown, but it takes Juliette's unusually low pitched voice to break me out of my trance.

"You like him don't you?" She asks standing directly behind me.

I bite my bottom lip in a moment of sheer panic and think very carefully about what the next words will be out of my mouth. Finally I turn around to face her once I think I've got my composure.

"He's not as bad as I originally thought."

"No, Elizabeth. I mean ... you're attracted to him aren't you?"

"What makes you think that?"

"Well there were a lot of giveaways tonight, but the biggest one is the fact that you're out here worried about what's going on in there." She points towards the office door.

"I'm just worried that my cousin and his father are arguing over something that I may have some small part in. That's all. I'm not sure what you think you are seeing, but that's it."

Aunt Juliette begins to laugh.

"What's so funny?" I demand to know.

"I said almost the same exact thing when your father and your uncles suspected the same thing about me and Joseph. Now I know you're lying. Either to me or to yourself."

"I'm getting the wine." I say walking away and back towards the kitchen. Fighting very hard not to reveal any I just got busted tears in front of my aunt.

"I'll get you a glass."

19

Roman

"I WANT to get back to my wife and the carrot cake that I know she baked for your ungrateful ass. So let's make this quick. No bullshit. What is going on between you and Elizabeth?"

Here we go.

"I didn't pay her because you weren't exactly clear about the terms, Joseph."

"I'm not a dumb fuck, Roman. I didn't build this life I have, that we have, from being stupid. I already know that you went to the Bahamas. And I'm pretty sure that if I send Elizabeth to Miami and New York that you'll conveniently have business to do in those places too. You're sniffing up her ass, and I want to know why."

"You told me to! She has a little problem with an ex that I'm taking care of. I found out he was in the Bahamas same time she was. So I flew out there and handled the problem like I always do. Per your orders."

"Then why did Jade lie to me about it?"

"Jade doesn't lie." I am calling his bluff like a motherfucker.

"She said you were away handling business."

"I was."

"She made it seem like it was Mendez business."

"I doubt that. That's probably what you assumed, but Mendez is taken care of already."

I hate this shit.

I just want to tell him already and deal with the inevitable fall out. I'm just hesitant about doing it until I have Elizabeth completely on board. I'm going to have to work a lot harder to get her to finally come around, because this shit is killing me. I've never had to lie to Joseph before. I just don't do it. I've never wanted him to think that his opinion matters enough where I'd ever need to.

"I never thought I'd need to say this but regardless of the lack of a blood connection, Elizabeth is your family. You do realize that, Roman?"

"Of course."

Joseph continues to silently stare down my throat, as I stand in the room in a defiant pose. I'm leaning on the door of the office with my arms crossed in front of me. It's obvious that I'm protecting something or someone. I've really handled all of this the wrong way. It's only going to be worse when I do finally tell him the truth. Maybe I should just fess up and apologize to Elizabeth later about exposing us without giving her a heads up. Fuck.

The bottom line is that she's mine, I want everyone to know it, and I'm never going to let any fucking body else have her. So the world is going to have to find that shit out sooner or later. Maybe I'm going to have to push her a little. Maybe I'm coddling her too much.

"I want to go eat my cake," Joseph announces.

"So go eat it. I think we're done here."

He pauses again as he watches me jiggle my hand

around in my pocket. I'm fingering a few M&M's, but I know he's watching me like a hawk, so I won't eat them.

"If I tell you where your mother is will you leave her alone?"

What. The. Fuck.

"You know where my mother is?"

"Yes."

My heart is fighting to burst through my chest. I'm so fucking mad that I really want to push the old man's head through his office window right the fuck now, but I have to use every bit of restraint I have from doing so. So I start pacing and talking myself down.

It's wrong Roman. He's your father. Get a fucking grip.

"Do you want to know where she is?" He asks as if he's almost amused by my reaction. As if he's enjoying it.

Shit, I'm not even sure if I want to know.

"How long have you known?"

"For a very long time. I have lots of connections from the old neighborhood, Roman. You know that. I've kept tabs on your mother for years."

"Why would you keep that shit from me?"

My mother has always been a source of tension between us. He knows that no matter how much I avoid the subject of my mother that I would still want to know where she is and how she is. The fact that he's been holding out on me is unforgivable, unless he has one hell of an excuse, which I highly doubt.

"Because she was never a good mother, and I thought I could do a better job, which I did. Telling you would have only confused things for you. You were already a handful."

In other words, fucked up.

"That wasn't your choice to make."

"I made it though."

"I'm a man now. You could have told me eventually."

"There didn't seem to be any reason in telling you after a certain point."

His nonchalant attitude is pissing me off, but that's classic Joseph. He lacks the ability to feel any sort of empathy for anyone. Even his own son. Sometimes I wonder if he's even able to feel love. Not that I'm any sort of expert on that emotion.

"Does she live close?" I ask.

Somehow knowing that she may have been living ten minutes away from me this entire time makes me even angrier.

"No, Roman. You don't get details until I get your word."

"This is very fucked up, Joseph."

"You're right it is. Elizabeth is your cousin not your whore. Do I have your word or not?"

I start rubbing my hand back and forth across the top of my buzz cut in frustration. The old man has got me by the balls, and I'm going to have to make a big decision about it right fucking now.

"You know what? You're right. She was a shit mom. I don't need to know where she is. I'm going to eat carrot cake and forget we even had this conversation."

And I walk out of the room.

"Juliette!" I call out.

Juliette walks quickly out of the kitchen with a glass of wine in her hand. Elizabeth directly behind her.

"What is it? Is everything all right?"

"Everything's fine. I heard you made a carrot cake." I plaster on a smile.

"I did." She grins proudly while looking around me for Joseph. "Would you like a slice?"

"I'd love a big hunk with some milk if you have it."

"Of course sweetie. Would you like some too, Elizabeth?"

"Sure I'll have a sliver."

"Elizabeth." I grab onto her wrist before she walks back into the kitchen. "Joseph and I just had a talk about your fee."

I say it loudly enough for Juliette's sake, although we didn't discuss shit about it.

"And?"

"Let's talk about it after cake."

"Okay." She says with a bit of uncertainty in her voice.

Joseph never came out of the office to eat dessert with us. The grumpy asshole. He and Juliette ate privately inside his office, while Elizabeth and I ate in the den while she caught up on an episode of some crappy reality show I've never heard of.

I pretty much grew up in this house, so I know the sound of the office door when it opens. It has a distinctive squeak. That's why I decide to take a chance and slide my hand underneath Elizabeth's dress. That and the fact that I've been dying to do it all fucking night.

"You can't be serious," she says with a stern look as she pushes my hand away.

"Oh I'm serious as a fucking heart attack." I growl.

"They are literally two feet away," she whispers angrily.

"I'm just checking." I smirk.

"On what?" She can't help but smile in response. She knows exactly what I'm talking about.

"On what's mine."

I gently slide my hand under her dress and in between her legs. I caress the insides of her thighs in a maneuver to coax her legs open for me. As soon as she cocks her legs open, I touch the edge of her panties and freeze.

"What do you have on?" I ask her.

"Your gift."

"Fuck me." I whisper to myself. This is straight torture.

I wish I could rip her dress off of her right now and get a full appreciation for how fantastic she must look, but I guess I'll just have to settle for this.

I slip the crotch of the silk and lace panties I gave her to the side, and then I slide my middle finger softly between her folds where I find her completely drenched. It's this right here that makes all Joseph's bullshit completely worth it.

I'm choosing Elizabeth.

I think I'll always choose her.

"Soaking wet," I say with approval as I slurp her juices off of my finger.

"Roman!" She protests half-heartedly.

"What? Did you want some?" I tease. Sliding my finger inside her mouth. Hooking it inside of her cheek and pulling her mouth to mine. "Kiss me, Duchess, and hurry up before we get caught."

She playfully slaps my chest, and slinks both her arms around my neck exactly where they fucking belong, then gives me a slow and languid kiss. A kiss that tells me that for a split moment she has forgotten exactly where she is. Which is two steps away from her aunt and my father. It's also a kiss that tells me that she's mine, that she knows it, and that there's no fucking turning back now.

I don't know exactly how it happened or when it happened, but I'm in deep with this girl, and it isn't just about the amazing pussy. For once in my life, it's so much more than that. I wonder if it could possibly be like that for her too.

When Elizabeth finally pulls away she playfully asks, "So I thought we were going to talk about my fee Masterson?"

"I'll pay you whatever the fuck you want." I grin.

"I don't want money."

"What do you want?" I grin hoping that it's my dick that she wants. That she always wants.

I hear the creak of the office door opening, curse under my breath, and move to the far side of the couch.

"What's wrong?" she asks.

"They're coming." I say quietly.

"We want to talk to you both." Juliette says in a voice I haven't heard since I was about sixteen years old. Clearly Joseph has been filling her in on his suspicions, and she isn't happy with the shit.

"What is it?" I say in defensive mode. Ready to do battle.

"Yeah, what is it?" Elizabeth says, and I'm a little surprised by her tone. Almost as if she's ready to do battle too. My little warrior. Maybe she is ready for this. For us.

"Elizabeth, I am not your mother or your father, and I do not represent them. This is a safe space for you to tell me anything." She pauses for effect.

"Okaaay," Elizabeth replies.

"So I'm just going to ask, is your ex-boyfriend stalking you?"

I look directly at Joseph as he smirks at me. This is his way of ratcheting up the heat, but still giving me an opportunity to take him up on his deal by not spilling everything that he thinks he knows. He doesn't want to tell Juliette what he suspects, but he's willing to guide her to her own realization about Elizabeth and me, if I continually refuse his order to leave her alone.

"No Auntie. What makes you think something like that?"

"You can tell the truth, Elizabeth. Roman has already told your uncle that he had to go to the Bahamas and handle a problem between you and your ex. Who is this guy? Is he part of the reason why you left your apartment?"

I can tell immediately by Elizabeth's body language that she's angry with me. She thinks I just went in that office and started blabbing all of her business. She should know me better than that though.

"He actually didn't have to come. I had it handled. And just for the record, it was pure coincidence that Ethan was there. He isn't stalking me."

"That's your story and you're sticking to it huh?" Juliette asks with turned up lips.

"That's the truth," Elizabeth says.

"Should we have an order of protection drafted just in case, Joseph?" Juliette asks the old man.

"Auntie—"

"Are you even listening to her?" I interrupt angrily. "Elizabeth just said she had it handled, and even if she didn't, I already went down there and made sure it was handled. Her ex won't be bothering her anymore."

"Stay respectful when you talk to my wife or there's going to be problems," Joseph warns.

"You started this shit by running your mouth about things that are Elizabeth's business, not yours."

"Enough!" Elizabeth shouts. "This has got to be one of the worst family dinners I've ever attended in my life. I thought my parents were a piece of work, but they've got nothing on you two seriously dysfunctional Masterson men. Roman, you should go. Auntie and Uncle Joseph, I'm going to start looking for a new place to live."

"Oh my God, Elizabeth, that's not what I want." Juliette cries. "I'm sorry. We shouldn't have brought up the stalking thing. I was just worried about you. Don't leave."

"That has nothing to do with it." Elizabeth moves next to Juliette's side. "I was going to move out soon anyway, Auntie. That's why I wanted to earn the extra money. I can't live on your kindness forever. This was always a temporary situation."

I smirk in Joseph's direction. He knows everything that I'm thinking right now with this one look on my face. Elizabeth moving out will only work in my favor. I'll have access to her without being under his watchful eye and maybe Elizabeth will learn to relax a little more and let what's happening between us just be.

"What about rent?" The old man asks cockblocking.

"I think the fee we worked out should cover her expenses for about three or four months don't you think, Joseph?" I grin.

Juliette looks at the old man expectantly. He notices the hopefulness in her eyes and in that moment makes the decision to back down.

"I suppose it will," he replies.

"Good," Juliette says. "I mean I definitely don't want you to leave, but at least I know you'll be okay until you get another job or God willing you get the investment."

"Thanks, Auntie."

Juliette and Elizabeth hug while Joseph gives me an icy glare. Fuck him. He knows where my mother is and never said a word. I don't owe him shit.

"Didn't Elizabeth ask you to leave, Roman?" Joseph reminds everyone in the room.

"I'm going. Got shit to do anyway." I say.

"Wait a minute." Elizabeth says grabbing my forearm.

"Yeah?"

"The two of us didn't *actually* discuss how much you were paying me. Remember you said we'd talk after cake?"

I grin in Joseph's direction.

"That's right I did say that."

"Maybe we can talk about it over a drink at The Lotus?"

My grin spreads even wider.

"That's a brilliant idea cousin. Let's go."

20

Elizabeth

I'M LYING COMPLETELY shit faced in the middle of Sloan's kitchen floor. She's been mixing and pouring cocktails; and I've been drinking just about whatever she's handed me tonight.

Pink drinks. Brown drinks. Clear drinks.

The room isn't quite spinning yet, but I'm frackin' sweaty as hell and this granite floor seems to be cooling down my blazing hot skin. So I'm staying right here.

"You need to clean the lights over your island." I giggle. "I see dead bugs in 'em."

"Uh that's gross, and please stop inspecting my damn kitchen while you're drunk off your ass."

"You need better cleaning people." I chuckle some more.

"I know you're in a pissy mood, Bitsy, but shut up!"

I think I'm a mean drunk. Or maybe I'm being such an ass because I received the call I've been waiting for today, and it wasn't what I wanted to hear.

Mr Lambert and the investment group decided to pass

on School Bucks, but of course wished me the best of luck with all my future endeavors, blah, blah, blah.

The worst part though was that he didn't even call me. He had his assistant Daniella do the dirty work and the tone of her voice as she delivered my death blow led me to believe that this was something that she in fact did on a regular basis. Almost as if it was a memorized speech that she was required to give to turned downed entrepreneurs everyday.

"Let's talk about something else." I say trying to veer our conversation away from dead bugs and negative phone calls.

"Okay." Sloan grins. "Let's talk about that Dear John letter you sent Jagger."

"Was it too over the top?"

"What do you mean?"

"I mean I didn't think he even liked me that much, so maybe that email was a bit presumptuous. I don't know. I feel weird about it now that I've sent it."

"Oh don't start back peddling now. You've got to own your shit. You sent it and it's done. Now the poor swimmer's heart is broken. Although I don't know why you did it. I thought we both agreed that he was good for you?"

"We did agree but things change. And shut up about his heart, Sloan. He probably could care less." I chuckle to myself, as Sloan's head starts to look like a lava lamp.

Gosh I'm drunk.

"Yes he does care and he's mad too, because he thinks you Dear John'd him because of Ethan."

"Why would he think that ridiculousness?"

"Because those two had some words. Some little birdie told Ethan that Jagger's been pushing up on you while he was away at *rehab*," Sloan says with air quotes. "And your ex didn't like it. The two of them had a little scuffle."

"Oh my God."

"I know right! You've got three hot guys fighting over you, and I can't even find one. Little does he know you probably Dear John'd him because of the third guy."

I ignore that last part of the comment and start rolling from side to side on the floor.

"I need crackers, Sloan. I didn't eat today."

She looks down at me incredulously. "Why because of that damn phone call?"

"That would be a hell yes."

"Oh please. Both you and I know that you could get that money from your uncle in a heartbeat or even easier from the Dark Knight."

"That's not the point. That's not how I wanted to get the money."

"Who the hell cares *how* you get the money, Bitsy? All that matters is that you do get it. That's business 101. And you and I both know that the Dark Knight will probably give you anything you want now that you've given him a taste."

For the last few weeks, I haven't exactly hidden the fact that I've been seeing Roman from Sloan. And like I figured she would, she disapproves. It's all in her tone of voice when she talks about him.

"Why don't you like Roman?"

"Who says I don't like him?"

"You're my best friend, Sloan. I know you. You don't like him. And where are my crackers?"

"Here." She flings a sleeve of saltines on my stomach. "And stop rolling around. Sit up before you throw up."

I sit up and prop myself up against the base of the counter. I tear open the package of saltines and start munching on one of the salty squares like it's a juicy ribeye steak.

"I am by no means a goody two shoes, Bitsy, but the guy is your cousin and more importantly he's kind of possessive not to mention dangerous."

"What is with everyone and this dangerous crap? I've never seen him hurt a fly." Well that's not entirely true.

"That doesn't mean he isn't capable of it."

"Well hell, I think you're capable of doing a lot of shit that you probably wouldn't do. Anyone is."

"You know what I mean. This is no college boy we're talking about. This guy is doing grown man shit. He doesn't want to date you, Bitsy. He wants to own you."

Even though I don't particularly like what she's saying, I understand exactly where Sloan is coming from. Regardless of how different Sloan and I are, in many ways we think just alike. I've always known that the best type of guy for me is someone square, someone smart, my age, who doesn't want anything too serious but isn't going to jerk me around either.

I know that guy is probably someone like Jagger, but I can't make myself want him. Not in the way that I want Roman. Although I just don't know if I'm ever going to be ready to own up to my feelings for Roman. I don't know if I'm brave enough.

The doorbell rings and Sloan looks over at the door in surprise.

"Who the hell could that be at this hour?"

I hear her walk up to the door and say under her breath, "Shit."

"Who is it?" I ask still munching on crackers.

"Did you drunk text him, Bitsy?"

"Who?"

"Your damn cousin!"

We both become startled at the two heavy raps at the door.

"No." I shriek. "Don't answer the door, Sloan. He can't see me looking like this."

"Are you serious right now? How does he know where I live anyway?"

"I don't know. I didn't tell him, but I didn't know it was a secret either."

"So you did tell him where I live?"

"I told you no, Sloan."

"Jesus Bitsy."

Another loud knock and a curt, "Open the door, Sloan."

Shit.

Sloan looks at me silently and widens her eyes as if to say, *"What do you want me to do bitch?"*

"Answer it. He's probably not going to go away."

When Sloan answers the door, Roman is standing in the doorway in all his magnificence. He's freshly shaved, dressed in all black, and has a look on his face that I'm not sure I've ever seen before. It's a cross between relief and annoyance … I think.

"Glamazon." He nods.

"Black Knight. I didn't realize you were coming over or I would have tidied up." Her words dripping in sarcasm.

"Wasn't planning on visiting, but plans change."

Roman saunters inside and over to me.

"What's this?" he asks me.

"I was hot," I say.

"Hot and drunk."

"Whatever." I wave him off.

"What's wrong with you, Elizabeth?"

"She didn't get the money." Sloan speaks for me.

Roman kneels down in front of me.

"I'm sorry, baby."

I get a strong whiff of Roman almost immediately. He

hasn't been drinking his usual Jack Daniels. Tonight he smells like a heavenly mixture of cognac, chocolate, leather and musk. Just like the night we met. It's a heady combination that's making me wish we were alone in his apartment, or his car, or any frackin' place other than here.

"It's fine," I say. "I'll figure something else out."

"Come on. I'm going to take you home."

"She can't go home like that!" Sloan exclaims.

"I got this, glamazon."

"She was going to stay the night here. There's no need to take her anywhere. I've got her."

Roman stares me directly in the eyes and lifts my chin with two of his fingers.

"You want to stay here and eat those dry crackers with the glamazon or come with me? I'll get you a nice turkey burger."

"Mmmm," I moan. A turkey burger would be fantastic right about now.

"From my favorite spot?" I ask excitedly.

"Yep," he answers me smiling.

"Where are her things?" he asks Sloan.

Sloan stares at me for a moment, sucks her teeth and goes to the bedroom to grab my overnight bag and my shoes.

"Here. You're a real credit to women everywhere, Bitsy." Sloan says sarcastically.

Roman grabs the bag then swiftly lifts me up and slides me around on his back.

"Hold onto my neck, Duchess."

"Oh brother." I think I hear Sloan mutter.

In fact that's about some of the last words I hear, as I drape the weight of my body completely on Roman's back and shoulders and fall fast asleep.

I awaken to warm sunlight and my completely nude body swaddled in eggplant purple sheets. Roman's purple sheets … but no Roman.

There's a bottle of spring water, a bottle of extra-strength Excedrin, and a folded note on the nightstand table next to me.

Take two pills. Drink the entire bottle of water. Don't move. I'll be home soon with your lunch.

Lunch? Oh crap, it's frackin' one in the afternoon.

After I follow Roman's explicit instructions, the next thing I do is look for my cell. I think it may be on the kitchen counter, so I get up wrapped in the sheet and make my way to the living room where I stop dead in my tracks. I don't know how I didn't hear them, but Jade, Cutter and Camden are all sitting in Roman's living room. And now they're staring, slack-jawed at me.

"Excuse me," I apologize. "I didn't realize you all were out here. I waaaaas–" I begin to stutter. "I waaaas drunk last night. I must have passed out in here."

"You got drunk with Rome?" Camden asks curiously.

"No with Sloan."

"So where is she?" Cutter asks looking around the room.

"She's not here. I think … I think that Roman brought me here from her house."

Camden and Cutter's smiles are growing wider and Jade's face stonier, as my story simply gets worse and worse. I just want to throw this sheet completely over my head and pretend that I'm invisible like I did when I was five. Where is an invisibility cloak when you need one Harry Potter?

All four of us turn our heads when we hear a key being

inserted into the front door. Roman enters the house with two bags full of diner food and my stomach growls as a salutation.

"Morning, glory. You hungry?" he asks me.

"Yes," I admit quietly.

"You may want to change first," Jade says to me.

"Right," I say on my way back to the bedroom totally embarrassed.

Gratefully Roman has access to his master bathroom from inside his room, so I don't have to do yet another walk of shame in order to take a quick shower. I know that I probably smell like vodka, gin, and hell. But before I go in, I decide that it wouldn't hurt to eavesdrop a little on what they're saying. I know it's about me.

"What the fuck Rome? Are you banging your cousin?" Cutter asks.

"That's none of your business," Roman replies.

"Well you invited us here for a meeting knowing good and well that she was here wrapped up in one of your sheets. So I think you've now made it our business," Jade says.

"Let me first apologize and say that I'm sorry if I misled any one of you into believing that my personal fucking life was up for discussion. It's not."

I think I hear the other brother Camden laugh out loud and speak next.

"So you want us to pretend that we didn't just see what the fuck we just saw?" he asks.

"That's right. Same way I pretend not to notice you staring at Jade's ass every time she walks by. Same way I pretend not to notice that Cutter has been Googling Elizabeth's glamazon friend like some pervert. Same way I pretend that Jade—"

"All right that's enough!" Jade cuts him off abruptly.

Then there's some additional laughter followed by silence.

I take that as my cue to go take a well needed shower and leave the friends to their standoff. I just pray that they are all gone by the time I finish. My stomach is grumbling, and I want that damn turkey burger.

After thirty minutes of lathering and scrubbing myself to death, I throw on the pair of black leggings and plaid blouse that I packed in my overnight bag, and sit on the edge of Roman's bed and brush my hair. Again and again and again.

I'm killing time.

I don't want to go back out there, because I'm not sure that they're gone, and I'm not ready to face them. There's a brief knock on the bedroom door and then Roman walks in with a plate of food.

"Your turkey burger is probably cold as ice. Do you still want it?"

"Are your friends still here?"

"Is that why you're hiding out in here?"

"Yes, Roman! Why would you tell them to come over for a meeting when I'm naked in your bed? I can't believe you."

"My business stops for no one, not even your pretty little ass." He kisses me hard on the lips.

"Roman," I mouth.

"All right let's talk real shit, Elizabeth."

"Okay."

"First take your food." He hands me the plate. "Eat it."

I take a bite of my burger and miraculously it's not freezing cold. It's still warm and at this point tastes like a lobster dinner.

"Good?" he asks.

"Yes," I moan.

"Good. Now for some real talk."

"All right."

"Do you enjoy my company, Elizabeth?"

"Yes."

"Do you enjoy the way I fuck you?"

"Oh my God, Roman … your mouth."

"Do you?"

"Yes okay?"

"Do you want more of the two? Spending time with me and fucking me?"

I'm taken aback at how very crass this *real* talk is.

"I'm pretty sure I do."

"Pretty sure? I want a hell yes or a hell no."

"Roman–"

"Not going to ask twice, Elizabeth."

"Hell yes." I mutter with more burger shoved in my mouth.

"Good we're on the same page then. I want the same. Which means that there are going to be times that my friends and business partners will be here and that you may also be here at the same time. You have to accept it and deal with it. They're not going anywhere and neither are you."

"Have they accepted it? I heard them talking about me out there. They didn't really sound like the were on board."

"They were just surprised."

"Jade too?"

"Jade is Jade. She just wants what's best for me, but she'll come around, and when she does she'll see that being with you is what's best for me."

"Does she have a thing for you?" I ask a little concerned that I've blindly wandered my way inside a love triangle.

"No," he chuckles. "I'm pretty sure she has a thing for

Camden. Not me, Duchess."

"Oh?"

"And what about your people?"

"What people?"

"Glamazon. Tiny. Jagger?"

"I talked to Jagger if that's what you mean. He knows that all we can be is just friends."

"Did you tell him it was because of me?"

"You know I wouldn't say anything about us. I haven't told anyone. The only one who thinks she knows everything is Sloan, and that's because I find it very difficult to hide anything from her. She knows me too well."

"Yeah that and the fact that she gets you drunk to get the rest of the info."

"Whatever," I roll my eyes.

"You know you didn't need to get drunk last night."

"Why not? I was sad. I wanted to wallow in it for a little while. That's what girls do."

"You didn't need to get drunk, because I'm going to give you the money. I'm your Plan B, and I don't want to hear shit else about it. When I saw you drunk and slumped on the ground like that last night, Duchess, I didn't like it. I don't want to ever see that shit again."

"Awww you were worried about me."

"Be quiet and give me your account number."

"I said I won't take your money."

"Calm your tits. I'm paying you for the work you did on the computer network. We'll talk about the other money later. In fact, you can give me the account info later."

"Why?"

"Because you've got a punishment coming, baby."

I smile and put the rest of my burger down.

"Yes, sir," I say as I give him a mock hand salute.

"Shut up and strip."

21

Roman

ELIZABETH'S BUTTER soft thighs are straddled across my face, my hands palming her plump ass, and my mouth front and center on her pussy. When I tilt my face up, I notice the filtered sunlight pouring in my bedroom and hitting the side of her in a way that is making the thin layer of sweat on her entire body shimmer.

She's so fucking pretty up there, I start imagining crazy shit like her riding my face just like this but wearing nothing else but a long, lace wedding veil and a fucking smile.

What. The. Fuck.

Just when my tongue starts giving her clit a few rapid flicks and she starts hitting her stride, someone's cell phone starts ringing.

Nonstop.

Whoever the hell it is that's calling one of us, keeps calling back, and it's distracting the fuck out of me. But Elizabeth either doesn't hear it or chooses not to hear it because her hips are still moving at a steady back and forth pace and her almond eyes are still blissfully locked on mine like the obedient sexy ass she is.

As if a fog has been lifted from my brain, it hits me that the ringer tone on the phone doesn't belong to me. It's an old phone tone that some use on their iPhones, but I never select that ring; and I didn't think Elizabeth did either. But maybe she's changed ringtones recently.

When Elizabeth comes for me it's always thunderous and exquisite to watch. I love to see the torturous look of ecstasy spread across her face and the sated feeling that washes over me right afterwards.

But that fucking phone.

It's still ringing. And since she just got off this time she notices. Without as much as a glance towards me she climbs down off of my face and goes for her phone.

"Hey," she says casually to whoever is on the other end.

Then she walks her little naked ass right into my bathroom, shuts the door, and proceeds to have a full blown conversation with the last person on earth that she should be speaking to.

That motherfucker.

"Okay, Ethan. Just let me get dressed and I'll meet you there in like a half hour."

If I hadn't just finished giving Elizabeth one of the best orgasms of her life, I'd seriously believe that there were cameras on me right now? This just has to be one of the craziest fucking pranks ever, because I know that she did not just hop off my damn face and take a call from that little shit. She can't be that damn stupid.

"Elizabeth!" I bellow as I proceed to kick down my fucking bathroom door.

SPLASH.

"Roman, wake up. Wake the frack up!"

"Fuck." I slide my palm down my face. It's wet. In fact

my whole face and pillow are wet. "What the fuck, Duchess?"

"You were having a nightmare. You were yelling my name like you wanted to kill me."

"Shit."

"What were you dreaming about?"

I scrub my hand across my face to help myself wake up. I drank a few too many lowballs yesterday and fucked my girl senseless for half the night. No wonder I'm out of it. I just don't know why I'm letting that fucker creep inside my head and into my sleep? Why the fuck am I letting this punk intimidate my subconscious? I should kick my own ass.

"Well?" She asks.

"Nothing but fucking you, baby."

"Really? Because I think you were trying to kill me when we were making love in that dream of yours. Should I be concerned, Neanderthal?"

"Is that what we do, Duchess? Make love." I ask holding back a chuckle and making her blush in embarrassment.

"Shut up, Masterson. You know what I mean."

"I wasn't literally killing you." I try to assure her with a lie. "I was killing the pussy."

"Humph." She crosses her arms and pouts. "You're lying."

"Come here."

"No, I'm tired and dirty … and you're a liar and wet."

I slip my hand between her legs.

"No, baby, you're the one who's wet. Now come here."

I think for a second about pulling Elizabeth on top of me and having her ride me for a while, but I realize that it will look entirely too much like the nightmare I just woke up from. So I decide to change up the scene, and pull her by the waist and up on all fours. Deciding that this will be a better way to fuck that jerk out of my system and hers.

Plus, she loves it like this.

"Masterson," she moans in that hypnotic voice of hers.

"Arch your back and turn your head so I can see you. Then I'll give you what you want."

Elizabeth does as she's told and as I slide hard and deep inside her from behind, I take a moment to relish in the feeling of complete rapture.

Total bliss.

In this moment, I'm not worried about shit except if I'm going to be able to hold off blowing my load before she does. When I'm inside her, I can almost forget about everything. And when I fix this little Ethan problem of mine, I will be able to *always* forget.

"Masterson!" She yelps after an especially deep stroke that hits her just where she likes.

"Don't you fucking come, Duchess." I order.

Although I have a lot of fucking nerve. I'm very damn close to coming myself, like I'm some sort of horny sixteen-year-old boy who's going for broke.

She lets out a few whimpers and slaps one of her palms on the headboard, that let's me know that she's concentrating really hard to follow the only rule I require in the bedroom. Of course it's the most difficult one for her to follow. Not to come unless I say so.

Actually I could probably stretch this whole scene out a bit longer on my end and have her break my rule, which is a whole other level of fun in and of itself. My orgasm punishments are my specialty. I've done them with plenty of women before I met Elizabeth, but there's something about carrying them out with her that's special.

I get in a zone when I'm in the middle of that shit with Elizabeth, and it becomes damn near a spiritual experience. She starts speaking in tongues, and I start thanking whatever higher being is up there for giving me her. For giving me *this*.

Oh shit.

Am I in love with her?

22

Ethan

"HAVE A SEAT, MR. ANDERSON."

Images of the movie *The Matrix* come to mind when the man in the cheap taupe suit says my name. He looks like one of the many special agents that I've met with over the last few months in the federal task force assembled to bring down the main syndicate running drugs in and out of Philadelphia. The Eighth Street Mafia. An organization that was born in the neighborhoods, grew in the jails, and has its reach spread wider than I ever imagined. The same crew I was selling drugs to college students for.

Unfortunately I'm not really interested in sitting with agent new guy for an hour in this sterile, cold room complete with metal table and hard chairs. Mainly because every agent I've met has had a hand in fucking up this case in a major way.

Vin was never ever supposed to be able to get close enough to me to do what he did. Following me to Elizabeth's apartment. Hurting her. Once he broke into Elizabeth's apartment I tried quickly texting Agent Suarez, the guy specifically assigned as my handler, but I didn't have enough time to give him any sort of concrete information. Just a quick text.

That's why I made sure to slide the phone under Elizabeth's bed before they got to us. If Vin had checked the phone he would have seen that Suarez had been calling me all night trying to check in with me, and that my only reply was a 911 text hours later.

If Vin had seen that, I would be dead, and so would Elizabeth.

"Who are you?" I ask more annoyed than anything else.

I don't trust these dicks anymore, but I have to play nice. Especially because my father pulled every string he had to keep me out of prison. After Vin took me from the house, I took him to a location that had already been designated by the task force as my supposed stash house. They rigged it with cameras and audio equipment weeks before, anticipating that Vin would eventually come after me; so it didn't take long for them to rush in and arrest him. Unfortunately there are a lot of fuckers who work for Vin and the task force had to put me under protection for a while after his arrest. Just until things cooled down.

I was never in Arizona. I had always been in the Bahamas under a sweet protection arrangement my dad finagled for me. It was pure coincidence that I saw Elizabeth there. Or maybe fate.

"I'm your new handler, Special Agent Keen."

I doubt there's anything special about you.

"Where's Suarez?"

"He's been assigned to another case."

"Sick of me was he?"

Agent Keen chuckles at my Yoda like comment with very little genuine humor in his eyes. It's refreshing to see that he doesn't want to be here as much as I don't want to.

Maybe I've turned into the case that agents get when they're being punished. Awesome.

"Vin is locked up. What else do you need me for?" I ask.

"Drug dealers have relationships with lots of people to get where they are in the food chain of their organization. There are still plenty of people in this city who know who you are and are probably curious as to why you went missing right after Vin was arrested. And of course why you're back."

"So you're saying I'm in danger here?"

"Basically that's what I'm saying."

"Why can't I put it out there that I was locked up for a while. Wouldn't that explain me being missing?"

Agent Keen scoffs. "Because they can easily check that out and discover that you weren't. They have plenty of friends in every local jail within a hundred mile radius. Maybe even two hundred miles."

He leans in closer to my face now with definite purpose.

"Listen, Mr. Anderson, I don't think it was smart of you to come back to Philadelphia, and it's definitely not a good idea for you to start any romantic connections with anyone."

"What are you trying to say?"

"I'm saying that you're here now, and I'm sure Vin's people already know that you're here. So there's no changing that. But what you can do is leave Elizabeth Hill alone. She already got hurt once because of you. Next time it could be worse."

"She's my girl. If I just leave her completely alone, that will look crazy suspicious too."

Plus I don't want to give that trader Jagger or that asshole cousin of hers the satisfaction.

"People break up all the time, Mr. Anderson. There's nothing suspicious about that. So let me be clearer. You are to have zero contact with Elizabeth Hill and all of her known friends and associates, or we will revisit all drug possession and intent to sell charges against you."

What the hell!

"Why do you care about Elizabeth? This makes no fucking sense."

"Your relationship with that girl almost compromised a case that we've been building for over thirteen months. All you need to do right now is keep your head low, swim for your country, and let us know if anyone else from Vin's old crew approaches you. That's it. That's your job. That will keep you out of jail Mr. Anderson and hopefully keep you alive."

I suck my teeth.

This is not what I want to hear on a Tuesday morning, but I guess I'm going to have to swallow my pride and deal with it. I moved back home to get my life back on track, and to be perfectly honest, all I really need to do is find a new piece of tail to get over the old. Preferably one already broken in.

Elizabeth was a cool girl, almost the perfect girl, but she was also a lot of fucking work.

She still is.

"I'll think about it."

"Wise decision, Mr. Anderson."

23

Roman

"WHY ARE we meeting in this shit-hole diner?" Camden asks. "How'd you even find this dump?"

"Shut up, they've got great turkey burgers."

"Turkey burgers? Who the fuck eats those?"

"Quiet asshole. Did you handle shit with Agent Keen?"

"Done."

"I owe you one, Cam."

"There's never any outstanding debts between us, Rome. You know that."

I knew the only way to get Ethan out of my head was to make sure that I eliminated him from Elizabeth's life once and for all. If I had it my way, he'd be resting quietly in a nursing home for the rest of his life with a tube down his throat. But that's the old me. The new me? Had to ask Camden to find out what that little prick was hiding, so that we could make him go away in a white collar crime kind of way.

"Was he difficult?" I ask.

"Not really. He has a wife, two kids and a mistress. He didn't want to fuck that sweet deal up. Plus he was more than willing to do it. Said the little prick Ethan and his daddy were a pain in the department's ass anyway. Least they could do was to make sure that your girl was taken care of."

Camden snickers. "I'm not ever going to get used to calling her that you know. Your *girl*."

"Get used to it, motherfucker."

"Has she gotten used to the idea yet?"

"I'm working on it."

"Every fucking night I bet."

24

Elizabeth

I'M SPITTING MAD.

That's why I've raided Sloan's closet and am wearing her super tight gold, cap-sleeved bandage dress and her gold fuck 'em girl pumps. I'm also permitting her to style my hair and make-up in whatever way she wants which is highly unusual for me, because I'm way more conservative than she is.

Tonight she's given me a sun-kissed, Miami-styled, makeover with a red lip. She's also washed my hair, worked product in it to smooth out the frizz, and then flat ironed it into a long, straight, glossy mane. It's not me, but I've got to admit, I look hot as hell.

After Sloan approves of her handiwork, she gets dressed, and we head out to a small lounge for a pre-birthday celebration. I'm turning twenty-four tomorrow, and a few of her co-workers are meeting us out for Friday night drinks. At a place that I'm pretty sure Roman knows nothing about. It's full of high-powered, high-strung, corporate types looking to unwind. Sloan is still on the hunt for her perfect corporate powerhouse husband and

I'm … I just want to be anywhere that I know I won't run into anyone I know. I just want to be someone else tonight, because sometimes I think that who I currently am is not who I ultimately want to be.

I was on a Target run the other day, and needed to check my bank account real quickly to make sure that I had enough funds to cover my purchase. I still haven't deposited the seventeen thousand cash that Roman gave me. I'm still deciding whether or not I'm going to keep it.

So anyway, I check my bank app and am frackin' floored to discover that my balance is not around one-hundred and thirty bucks like I assumed, but rather it's teetering over the twenty-five thousand dollar mark. After choking back a sip of my hot caramel macchiato and then paying for my purchases, I started calling Roman, before I could even roll my red shopping cart out to the parking lot.

"Duchess."

"What the frack did you do!?"

"Calm your tits baby. What are you talking about?"

"There's twenty-five thousand dollars in my bank account, asshole."

He laughed a little too heartily for my taste.

"Most women would be happy they had that much in the bank."

"Women who earned it."

"I highly doubt that would matter, Duchess. Plus you earned every penny."

"The job I did was not a twenty-five thousand dollar job. I didn't even go to Miami or New York to do the check-in's there."

"Now you know there was no way in hell that I was going to let you go to either of those places without me, and Joseph's been watching me like a hawk, so per your instructions we took care of everything from Philly, baby."

"Stop speaking to me in that patronizing tone," I barked.

"I paid you what the job is worth. Did you even do your home-

work on what jobs like that pay, Duchess? If we had hired a full-timer with experience to do the job, we would have paid at least seventy thousand a year. And that's low-balling it. This way we got the job completed for a fraction of the cost; we didn't have to pay you any health insurance and shit. Plus the icing on the cake was I received a stellar blow job to celebrate when you finished. That alone was worth the twenty-five grand in my opinion."

"You're such a pig and a liar," I sighed realizing I was probably fighting a losing battle.

Roman was in all likelihood right about the salary. I didn't do my homework about salaries in network and computer administration, because it was never anything that I was seriously going to pursue as a career.

I've always known (or at least believed in my heart) since high school that I would be a tech entrepreneur, not a salaried employee. But that's not the point. That's not why he gave me this money. He and I both know this is his way of back-dooring his way into giving me the investment money that I've been looking for.

I don't know why he doesn't get it. He's practically been taking care of himself since he was a kid. I just really want to be able to say that I did this one thing on my own. Then he can spoil me all he wants.

"I don't lie, Elizabeth. That's for all the little sheep out in the world who are afraid of consequences. I'm a wolf. We're predators, not casualties."

"Oh please. You lie to Joseph everyday about all kinds of crap."

"What the hell are you talking about, Elizabeth? Are you inferring that I lie to him about me and you?"

"Well that's one of the things."

"I'm lying because you asked me to! I'm doing it for you."

"I know that. I'm just saying ... that you lie."

"You know what, I don't want to talk about this shit anymore. What do you want to do for your birthday Saturday?"

"Nothing with you, Daddy Warbucks."

"This shit again. You got a problem with how I earn my money Elizabeth? Is that why you won't take it?!"

"I've told you a thousand different ways that I want to do School Bucks on my own. How do I need to say it so that you can receive it? In Spanish? In sign language? In frackin' Klingon!"

"Keep raising your nerdy voice to me and see what happens, Elizabeth."

"What!? What's going to happen? Are you going to sucker punch me too like you did Ethan?"

"What the fuck did you just say?"

"You heard me."

Click.

The jerk hung up on me, and I haven't seen or heard from him since. He's such a damn baby.

So like I said … I'm spitting mad.

I haven't texted him, looked for him or asked about him. My job networking the computers has been long over, so there's no chance of me running into him that way; and he hasn't been by the house.

And you know what? It's been frackin' peaceful without him running rough shot all over my life. Ordering me around. Forcing money down my throat. Dictating when I can have an orgasm for God's sake.

"So when we get in there I want you to look at the guy with the goatee."

"He's your next victim?"

"My future husband you mean?"

"Yes ma'am that's exactly what I meant," I chuckle.

I've met some of Sloan's co-workers before. Three men and one woman. All of them sales reps for the pharmaceutical company she works for. One of the guys, Thomas, has always been a bit of a flirt with me and every other woman breathing. Nothing serious with me though, because he knows that I'm well aware that he has some poor unsuspecting girlfriend at home waiting for him.

"Ladies," Thomas drawls with some sort of fake southern accent. Sloan says it helps him with sales. Something about the gatekeepers at all the doctor's offices having a hard time saying no to the gentleman from down south.

"Hey Thomas," We both respond and he smiles extra hard at me. I'm figuring it's the dress.

"You look fan-fucking-tastic, Miss Hill."

"Thanks, Thomas."

"Buy us a round of drinks, Thomas." Sloan says while she nods a hello at the mystery hot guy with the goatee. He is definitely not one of her coworkers. He looks like a professional athlete. Built, extra tall, wearing a man-bun, and sexy as hell.

"What are y'all drinking?"

"Well it's Elizabeth's birthday tomorrow. So shots are probably in order don't you think?"

"Shots it is then. A preference, Elizabeth?"

"Maybe lemon drop shots." I say.

"Sure thing, Miss Hill," Thomas grins.

Oh brother, this is going to be a long night.

I feel a buzz going off inside my clutch bag. It better not be he who will not be named.

Nope, it isn't.

Mom: Where are you sweetie?

Me: Out mom. It's Friday night and my bday.

Mom: Your birthday is tomorrow. I should know, I was there.

Me: Haha mom.

Mom: Your father and I are coming there for dinner.

Me: Where?!

Mom: Juliette's. She's cooking you dinner right?

How does she frackin' know that already?!

Me: Juliette called you?

Mom: Yes is there a problem?

Me: Joseph. Dad.

Mom: They're grown men sweetie. They know how to act civilized for a few hours. We'll be there at seven. Have fun tonight.

Ugh!

Me: Bye mom.

"Here you go, Elizabeth."

Thomas hands me a shot glass and I gladly accept. I'm ready to numb myself and forget that I'm probably about to bring in the crappiest birthday I've had yet.

"Thanks, Thomas."

After about twenty minutes, two rounds of shots, several laughs, and some random chit-chat with Sloan's friends, Thomas gets around to asking me to dance. He's innocent enough, and I'm tipsy enough, so I accept.

There's a small dance floor in the center of the room with two couples already dancing, and by the time we arrive on the dance floor the song changes from a radio dance record to a slower one. Sort of reminds me of the first time I danced with Roman at Joseph's party. Gosh, that seems like forever ago.

I feel kind of self conscious now that everyone has a bird's eye view of me and Thomas on the dance floor, and when he pulls me in tightly to dance slower, I decide to go with it. I don't necessarily want to, but I don't want to make a big deal about it either.

Thomas feels nothing like Roman.

That's the first thought that enters my head when I clasp my arms gently around his neck. Why do I constantly compare every man that I run across to Roman? It's so annoying.

"You okay Elizabeth?" Thomas asks.

I'm sure he can feel the tension running through my body. Not only does he not feel like Roman, but he doesn't smell like him either. He smells like vodka. This doesn't feel right at all to me, and I'm only dancing. I can't imagine if I try to sleep with somebody else. That damn Neanderthal has cursed me.

"I like this song," Thomas says in my ear.

I smile and nod in agreement. "Me too."

"You want another shot?" He asks probably as an attempt to loosen me up.

"No but a drink would be good. Anything with vodka in it. I like to drink the same type of liquor all night. Had a bad experience mixing stuff not too long ago."

"Gotcha. Why don't you go sit back down, and I'll bring a vodka martini over for you."

"Thanks, Thomas."

I watch as Thomas's body becomes swallowed by the thirsty crowd at the bar. Twenty minutes later he isn't back yet, and Sloan is pissed.

"Where did that jerk go? If he was going to leave, he could have at least closed his tab. Now we're going to have to pay for it."

"Maybe his girlfriend called and he had to go." I say, but I'm not sure I believe my own words. I have a bad feeling about this.

"Uh, so the hell what. He could have said good-bye. I'm going to kick his ass Monday morning."

Everyone at the table laughs as if this is something that Thomas has done before, and even though I try to relax, I just want to double check that nothing bad has happened to him. I just have a feeling.

"Did Thomas drive?" I ask the table.

"Yeah the lucky asshole found a spot directly across the street. He drives a silver Lexus."

"I'm just going to check and see if it's there," I say.

"No, Bitsy, it's your birthday chica. One of these bozos can look for him. Right, Matt? Right, Alex?"

"His girl probably reamed his ass out and he had to go home. He's fine." Matt says. "I'm not wading through this crowd and going out there to see that his car is gone like we already know it is."

Sloan's new sexy friend with the goatee, Todd, grabs her wrist and gestures for her to have a seat next to him, which completely distracts her from the Thomas conversation, and essentially ends it. So I excuse myself to go to the bathroom.

After freshening up my lipstick and scrunching my hair with my hands to make sure it behaves the rest of the night, I decide that a little peek out the front door wouldn't hurt. I just want to see if his car his gone. I tell security that I'll be five minutes, so that he'll know to let me back in and he gives me a head nod in understanding.

Not twenty seconds after I step onto the sidewalk, I feel a familiar prickling sensation across the back of my neck. I look swiftly to my left and to my right for the source, but I don't see anything but random, strange pedestrian faces. I make sure to take a long sweeping glance up and down and across the street, but I don't see a silver Lexus either.

Maybe he did go home.

I'm probably worrying for no reason. He's a big boy.

I see a small mini mart store open on the corner and decide to make a quick run to buy a pack of mints and some gum before I head back inside. I toss my stuff on the counter and am checking inside my bag for some singles when someone walks directly behind me and up on my ass.

I freeze like a deer caught in a pair of headlights.

"You looking for your fucking boyfriend?"

Roman.

My blood begins to race. A reaction to his voice … a voice laced with fury.

"What are you doing here?"

Roman says nothing but places a ten-dollar bill on the counter, grabs my items, and pulls me outside. He pulls me around the corner where his Range Rover is parked. He unlocks the doors and orders me to get inside with a silent finger point.

"I'm out with friends," I say standing my ground. "I'm not getting in. Especially with someone who has nothing better to do than to stalk me."

"This lounge you were in just now, where you were slow dancing with some lame motherfucker, belongs to a friend of mine."

"And what? You were here by coincidence? You expect me to believe that."

"Hell no. He called me and told me you were here."

"Why!"

"He knows you belong to me. He knew I'd want to know that you were okay. I came because I needed to put eyeballs on you myself. I'm a hands on type of boyfriend."

"Boyfriend!"

"I didn't stutter."

"You must be smoking meth or something. I am *so* not your girlfriend. I'm not even your friend right now."

"Why did you leave your little party?"

"To get some gum."

"By yourself in the middle of the night? Maybe you're the one who's on drugs. Or are you really out here looking for your other little boyfriend?"

"Were you watching me in there?"

"Yep."

"How long this time?"

"Long enough."

So he saw me with Thomas. No wonder he's angry. My eyes shift anxiously.

"I saw you dancing. Flirting. Letting that prick touch you in this piece of a dress, which you look hot as shit in by the way. And guess what? I didn't sucker punch him like I should have. Like I could have. Like you'd expect me to."

All right maybe I deserved that. The Ethan comment I made the other day was a low blow. But that's besides the point.

"Did you see him leave?"

"Are you seriously still looking for *him* in the middle of our conversation?"

"What did you do, Roman?"

A bone chilling smile spreads across Roman's face.

"What do you think I did?"

"I don't know. What did you do? Where's Thomas?"

"Thomas, huh?"

Roman backs me up against the driver's side door of the Rover and the crazy Neanderthal has the nerve to be hard as a rock. I refuse to let that distract me though. Thomas could be lying in an alley somewhere gasping for his next breath, and I would be partly responsible.

"Get in the fucking car, Elizabeth."

"No!"

I reach in my purse for my phone. I'm going to text Sloan to come out and get me.

"I swear to fucking God if you text someone sitting in that club right now, I'm going to strap you to my bed for a week."

"You don't use straps you fake ass Dom!"

"There's a lot I haven't shown you yet, Elizabeth, but best believe I will when the time is right."

I start breathing heavily as Roman weighs his massive body heavily against me, leaning his forehead against mine.

"I missed the shit out of you, Duchess."

I close my eyes as Roman slides his right hand around the back of my thigh and hitches it up. My dress sliding up with it.

"I saw you in this dress and I wanted to kill every motherfucker in that place. They were all staring at you. Plotting on what's mine."

"Masterson," I say reverently.

"Did you miss me?" Roman's voice cracks just slightly, and I smell the chocolate on his breath. He's been eating M&M's.

He missed me.

I wrap my arms around Roman's neck and palm the back of his head like I do when we make love. I whisper softly on his lips, "Yes."

And I feel a smile spread across his.

"Happy birthday, Duchess."

I just notice that it's a few minutes past midnight.

"Thank you, Masterson."

"Let's go back to my place and bring that shit in right."

"I have to be back at the house tomorrow by no later than five," I warn.

"Whatever you want, baby. I just need to be inside you in the worst fucking way. I don't care how long you give me."

I kiss him after that.

Long, slow and deep the way he likes it.

He picks up my other leg and is holding me up against the car with one hand while never breaking the kiss. With the other hand, he smoothly unlocks the door, and before I know what's happening he's walked around the car and slides me inside the passenger seat.

Then he breaks the kiss.

"Text the glamazon and tell her you've gone home."

"All right," I say still a bit dazed from the kiss.

"Elizabeth."

"Yes?"

"I didn't hurt your boy Thomas. I just strongly suggested that he never dance with you again. He's the one that decided to leave the club."

I exhale a sigh of relief. "He's just a friend."

"Elizabeth."

"Yes, Roman?"

"Are we finished fighting about the money?"

"Do you understand why I was so angry?"

"I do but you also need to realize your worth. You are worth so much more than twenty-five thousand dollars, Elizabeth. You should never argue that point with me or anyone else."

I'm quiet after that.

He just schooled me and complimented me in one breath. We ride home to Roman's penthouse in heavy charged silence.

It's a ride filled with anticipation and sparks of electricity as I gaze outside of the car window, delightedly humming happy birthday to myself. My whole outlook has completely done an entire one-eighty.

It's going to be a good birthday.

25

Elizabeth

JULIETTE IS ON SPEED TEN.

She's been flitting around the house all morning like a housewife on Ritalin. Dancing to old house music, yapping on her phone, baking all sorts of yummy smelling desserts, and running errand after errand. She has got to be more excited about my own birthday than I am. That and the fact that I think she may be a little anxious about my father coming to visit. I think her jumpiness is starting to piss my uncle off though.

"Would you please calm down." He says to her while he places one of his palms on her cheek in a loving way.

"I am calm."

"I'd tell you to drink a glass of wine, but it's only one in the afternoon. I don't know why you're acting like the Pope is coming to dinner."

Juliette glares at my uncle with a little hurt in her eyes.

"My brother and his wife are coming for their only daughter's birthday. I haven't seen them in ages. I just want everything to be perfect. Do you have a problem with that Joseph Michael Masterson?"

"Oh so you're using my middle name now?" he chuckles. "I better watch it."

"That's right you better!" She says as she gives him a quick kiss on the lips. A gesture that seems to placate my uncle, because he gives her a quick swat on the ass in return and then walks back into his office with a smile.

They're so adorable.

"I think you have Uncle Joseph wrapped around your little finger." I acknowledge respectfully, because I can't figure out for the life of me how she does it.

How do you control a Masterson man? Or maybe I'm dealing with the younger, wilder version of Uncle Joseph. Perhaps Roman will calm down in about twenty years.

I laugh to myself.

Probably not.

"We've been together a long time sweetie. Each of us is wrapped around the other's finger," she says while wiping down the kitchen counters.

"Was it always like that between you two or was it something that grew?"

Juliette drops the antibacterial wipe she was using in the trashcan and turns towards me.

"It's your birthday, Elizabeth, so you can't lie. Are you asking me about Joseph or are you asking me about Roman?"

I'm not sure where my crazy aunt gets these rules of hers; of course I can lie on my own frackin' birthday.

"Obviously I'm talking about Uncle Joseph," I respond with a look of feigned mortification.

She grins. "You came in pretty early this morning."

"Birthday celebration." I respond a little too quickly.

"What did you do?"

"Hung out with some of Sloan's work friends."

"Oh? I've never heard you mention anyone really but

Sloan and that other girl. The one who's a little on the chunky side."

"That's Tiny."

"Interesting name."

"Yeah," I giggle.

My heart jumps at the double knock coming from the front door. Juliette's checking on some sort of pie in the oven, so I offer to grab the door.

"I'll get it."

"Thanks, honey."

I open the door to a grinning Roman.

"Happy birthday, Duchess."

Seeing him standing there in all his badass glory just makes me relive the last twelve hours, and I can't help but smile in response.

"Thank you, Roman."

"Roman is it now?" He asks in an amused tone while walking through the threshold.

I roll my eyes back at him playfully.

I think I may have called out his last name about a hundred times last night. That's how unbelievable the sex was between us. That's how passionate it always is. And I know I don't have much past experience to pull from, but something tells me that this isn't common or typical. Not if I go by some of the stories Sloan tells me about her sexcapades. Sure, she has a lot of fun, but there's never been a man that's ruined her for all the others.

That is what Roman is to me. Someone who's ruined the possibility for any others to come after him.

"I'm here to take you out for the day."

"I can't," I respond looking confused. Didn't Juliette tell him?

"Why?"

"My parents are coming for dinner. Juliette's been baking all morning. Didn't she tell you?"

"What time?"

"Seven."

"I'll have you back way before then."

"Roman, is that you?" Juliette calls from the kitchen.

"Yes, gorgeous."

"I swear I don't understand why you never use your key."

"Just trying to be respectful of your privacy. Never know what you and the old man could be doing in here," he jests.

I knock him on the shoulder with my fist.

"You're so gross," I say.

"Yeah, Roman, you're so gross." My uncle rumbles suddenly as he enters the room.

"Whatever Joseph. Listen I'm taking the birthday girl out for an hour or so."

"Is that right? Juliette come out here please."

Juliette walks in the living room while wiping her hands on a kitchen cloth.

"What is it?"

"I'm taking Elizabeth out for a few hours. I'll bring her back in time for your *little family* dinner." Roman emphasizes the words little and family with disdain.

A look of shame crosses my aunt's face then irritation.

"Joseph, honey, didn't you invite Roman to the dinner tonight?"

"Did you tell me to?"

"I thought it was understood," she says curtly. "You talk to him every other day about business, I thought you'd mention it in passing."

"Oh, I thought you would have texted him or something. Roman and I don't talk about personal stuff when we're meeting about business. But you're more than welcome to join us, Roman. Elizabeth's parents will be here for the night. Should be lots of fun."

There's no mistaking from the tone of his voice that he'd rather pull splinters from underneath his fingernails than break bread with my father.

"Well he doesn't have to—" I start saying to give Roman an out. I don't know if I want him here to witness the carnage that may take place over dinner. Not after I made such a stink the other night about all the Masterson dysfunction.

"What time should we be back for dinner?" he asks with a steely look in his eyes.

"Dinner starts at seven, but my brother is always early, so maybe you two should be back here by no later then six," Juliette says.

"No problem. We'll be here. You ready, Elizabeth?"

"Um … where are we going?"

"It's a surprise."

"Do I need to change?"

All I have on is a crisp white v-neck T-shirt and a pair of my favorite jeans. Luckily I did make sure to style my hair and put on a little make-up.

"Nope. You're fine."

"All right," I look at Juliette and Joseph. I can't read their faces right now, but I don't think it's good. "I'll be back on time. I swear," I assure them.

"Mm-hmm," My uncle mutters.

"You better," Juliette says right after that.

"Why is Mr. Tibbs in the car?"

"He missed you."

"Seriously? He hates me. I think he wants to eat me."

"No, I want to eat you," he teases. "Unbutton those jeans right now."

"What!"

"I need to do a spot check."

"You are ridiculous and in front of Mr. Tibbs no less," I complain as I actually do the ridiculous and unbutton my jeans in the middle of broad daylight in his Range Rover.

"He likes to watch."

Roman is parked a few cars away from the house, so even if Juliette peeked out the window, she wouldn't see us, but plenty of her neighbors definitely would. Neighbors that she's quite friendly with.

I stress about it for literally only ten more seconds, until Roman slides his right hand down and inside the front of my jeans. He uses four of his fingers to spread my thighs apart and his middle one to slide and dip inside of me.

"Warm and wet. Tell me, Duchess, did you get wet the moment you saw me at the door? Or was it something I said after that?"

He continues to slide and dip deeper inside of me and I can feel every ridge on the rough pads of his fingers.

"Shit," I mumble and moan simultaneously under my breath.

"What's that?"

"The moment I saw you at the door."

"I see."

I'm getting braver the more I'm with Roman and his fingers feel so good right now, I slide my hand over and grab in between his legs. His cock is brick hard, and I start wondering the same thing about him.

"Has your dick been this hard since I answered the door or was it something I said?" I ask breathlessly as he continues to rapidly move his finger across my clit.

"My dick stays hard for you twenty-four seven, Duchess," he growls. "That's it baby. Fuck you're still tight as shit. I must not be working this pussy hard enough."

"Masterson," I exhale harshly from his dirty words and his fancy finger work. One of my hands is gripping the handle on the side of the door tightly, the other is holding on to his massive bulge for dear life.

"Come for me, baby."

My muscles start trembling and the turbulence of my increased heart rate is either going to kill me or … kill me.

I pop my eyes open and look straight into his shiny ink black ones and when he says the word, "Now."

I scream.

And then I shudder and tumble down into what it feels like to come slowly down off of a Masterson orgasm. There's a distinct afterglow. With his lips, his hands, or his cock … it doesn't matter. It all feels absolutely spectacular before, during and after.

"Happy birthday, baby," he chuckles while sucking me off of his fingers.

So frackin' nasty.

"Thanks," I say fixing my hair and my clothes in a daze. "Is this why you came to kidnap me today?"

"Are you complaining?"

"No but–"

"Don't worry, I didn't just bring you out for this, but I can't lie, Duchess I love to watch you come. It's one of my favorite things to do."

I smile. "So where are you taking me?"

I turn my head towards the backseat to check on Mr. Tibbs. He's completely knocked out or severely unimpressed with our performance.

"Well I have a little celebration of my own."

"Yeah?"

"Remember that big client I told you I was working on?"

"The basketball player?"

"Baseball."

"Right baseball. His name was … Mendez."

"That's right. Well his interview went off without a hitch, so we finally got paid."

"Oh that's great, Roman! Was it a lot of money?"

"Yes. An obscene amount of money. So don't bug the fuck out when I show you your birthday gift. Remember that I can afford it. Remember that you're worth it."

I can't imagine what this nut ball has gone and bought me now, but I can tell by the lead up that I'm probably not going to like it very much.

While Roman starts driving towards our destination, he turns his palm up and lays it flat on the arm rest in between our two seats. It's the first time he's ever done this; and I'm pretty sure it's his way of asking me to hold his hand. I stare at him a bit blankly, and he gives me a quick return glance then another to his hand, so I place mine inside of his. And then he clasps our fingers together and smirks.

This is definitely headed into serious relationship territory, and I don't think I could stop myself even if I wanted to. It just feels too damn good. He feels too good.

After about fifteen minutes of driving in traffic, Roman pulls into the lot of a small commercial property near South Street.

"We're here."

"What's this?"

"This is a building I just bought."

"Umm … that's nice, but how is this a birthday gift for me?" I ask pausing to consider the look on his face.

"Come on inside."

I hold onto the the leather leash, as both Mr. Tibbs and I stand quietly by while Roman uses about three different keys to unlock the storm door and then a second heavy metal door behind it. I walk in and am amazed by the space. Like many commercial spaces in this area, you don't know how spectacular it really is until you get inside.

There's a huge open space with a massive loft area that spans the entire width of the building. There are also two separate moderately sized offices, as well as a third smaller room off to the side. There is a full bathroom complete with stone floors and tile. It's absolutely gorgeous. But I'm still confused.

"You like it?" he asks.

"It's amazing, Roman."

"Well I'm glad you think so, because it's the new head-quarters of School Bucks."

I damn near choke on my own saliva.

"What!"

"An office for you, the other office for your full-time coder, the loft space you can use as your bedroom; and maybe you can use the smaller room as a closet or something."

I'm stunned speechless and I decide to think really carefully about what I'm going to say next. I know he did this as a gesture of affection, and not just because he likes to throw his money around, because that's not him. But accepting a huge gift like this from him means a lot of things. Particularly that I'm going against the very thing I said I'd never do. Funding and building my business completely on my own.

"I know what you're thinking, Elizabeth, but listen. It's still on you to find the money to pay the coder and anyone else you hire. It's still on you to pay the taxes and upkeep on this place. And if it really is fucking with you; you can buy me out when the business starts turning a profit."

Roman walks up behind me and encircles me in his embrace.

"Until then, just accept this for what it is, a gift for my girl."

I squeeze my eyes tightly, not completely understanding, why I'm fighting back tears that are threatening to flow.

Do I love this man?

"Thank you, Roman." I turn inside his embrace and tilt my head up to face him. "This is the sweetest thing anyone has ever done for me. No wait, sweet isn't the right word. I just–"

"I get it, Duchess."

His mouth begins to kiss the salty tears away from around my eyes.

"Will you accept my gift?" he asks solemnly, and I know for sure that it's a loaded question.

Will I accept this building?

Will I accept him?

Will I accept everything that comes with ... loving Roman Masterson?

I tug on his T-shirt and pull him in closer to me. We begin kissing slowly, leisurely, silently. His tongue exploring my mouth as if it's searching for an answer to his question. When I think he's about to start asking me again, I slowly slide one of my fingers inside his mouth to shut him up and instinctively he pulls and sucks on it.

With my free hand I slide it under his shirt, running my fingers over his taut washboard abs and his chiseled pecs, sending what I think is a slight chill through his body. He enjoys my touch just as much as I crave his.

My finger pops out of his mouth and he pulls his shirt

up and over his head. Then mine. He quickly unfastens my jeans and yanks them down.

"Step out," he orders.

I step out of my jeans, kick them to the side, then wrap my arms around his neck as he lifts me up and against one of the walls in this vast empty space. I decide to do the honors and slide my bra straps off my shoulders so that he has easy to access to my breasts. He swiftly lifts me a smidgen higher and encloses his very warm and delicious mouth on my left breast and pulls hard.

I gasp.

"The only fucking sounds I want to hear out of your mouth are the words I accept. No moaning, no screaming, and definitely no coming until I say so. Are we clear, Duchess?"

I nod quietly.

"Good job, baby. Now hold on. I can't fucking wait to get inside you."

I hold onto Roman's neck and waist tightly with my arms and legs while he unfastens his jeans and slides them and his pair of black boxers down.

"My test results finally came in this morning. I'm clean. Can we skip the rubber?" He asks in a thick, heavy voice that's almost impossible to resist. Lucky for both of us, I want him inside me bareback just as much as he does.

I grin and nod in agreement. His eyes start to dance like I've given him the best present ever on Christmas morning.

He kicks his clothes to the side, slightly bends his knees, then lowers me slowly onto the thick, wide tip of his cock. Something about the angle of this position makes me feel extra full and it takes every ounce of strength the good Lord gave me not to yelp out his name in vain.

He continues to ram up inside me over and over while

I bury my face in the side of his neck to muffle my sounds of pleasure; and while I love how he's making me feel, I also want to kick his bossy ass for this bullshit quiet rule he's laid down. I guess I didn't realize how sex without a condom was going to make things feel better times frackin' infinity.

"I can't!" I scream.

"You can't what." Roman grunts as he continues to bang my brains out against the wall of what I think is now my new home.

"I. Can't. Be. Frackin. Quiet."

Roman pulls his head back and grins with smug satisfaction. "I know. So say the shit I need to hear."

"I–"

He thrusts up and deep and it knocks the wind out of me for a moment. I try speaking again.

"I … accept."

"Finally," he grunts.

"Now can I come, Masterson?" I practically beg.

"Yes, baby. Right the *frack* now."

And for the first time ever, Mr. Tibbs and I have a mutual meeting of the minds, and we both howl over the next few minutes in tandem.

I'm howling in utter ecstasy.

He's probably telling me to shut up.

26

Elizabeth

I'M in a house with a variety of characters. Two men that look like they'd rather be anywhere but here. One man that I'm sitting next to who keeps looking at me like a piece of chicken. And two women that keep bringing out enough dishes and desserts that could they feed a third world country.

Everyone is trying to be on their best behavior especially Roman. I can tell that he's trying to make a good impression on my parents, and I love him more for the effort, although I fear that it's all in vain. My father is still staring at him suspiciously out of the side of his eyes.

"Dinner was delicious as usual, Juliette," Roman says.

"Thanks, sweetie. Would anyone like coffee?"

"Oh I'll help you with that," my mother offers.

But the minute the two of them leave, something in the air quickly alters.

"So, Elizabeth, where did Roman take you for your birthday today?" Joseph asks.

I'm a little taken aback by the question. It came out of nowhere and after he says it, I notice the change in Roman's entire posture. Based on the timing of the question, it's almost as if Joseph is picking a fight for my father's benefit or maybe I'm just being paranoid. Maybe he's just genuinely curious.

"Umm … well," I swallow thickly.

"I took her to her new house."

"New house?" My father asks.

"Well–"

"How is that a birthday activity?" Uncle Joseph interrupts.

"Because I bought it for her as a birthday gift."

Dead silence.

"Okay here we go. Coffee's ready." Juliette interrupts then stops talking when she notices the looks on everyone's faces.

"What could have possibly happened in the three minutes that I was gone?" she demands to know.

"Seems that your boy here bought my daughter a new place." My father stands up and away from the table. "And I'm not understanding why."

My mother sets the mugs of coffee she was holding down on the table and stands next to my father, looking between Roman and me in confusion.

"What's going on, Elizabeth?" she asks.

Aunt Juliette's eyes are focused on the floor because of course she knows. She's known for a long time. She's given me multiple opportunities to come clean, and now I've dragged this thing out and it's imploding on my own damn birthday.

That's when Roman lays his palm face up on the table. Practically banging it there with force. Somehow the power with which he executes this one action injects me with the confidence I need to face the firing squad. So I place my hand inside of his and gather the courage to finally speak.

"Roman and I are together," I say.

"WHAT!" My father slams his hand on the table. "What the hell are you talking about?"

"Please calm down." My mother tries to shush my dad. "Let her finish."

Uncle Joseph is sipping his mug of black coffee quietly watching the whole scene he's orchestrated unfold and it's pissing me the frack off.

"What the hell, Uncle Joseph? Why did you start this on my birthday?!" I demand to know.

He stops mid sip. "I told Roman to leave you alone and he didn't listen. Maybe he'll listen to your parents."

"You knew this shit was going on?" My father asks Uncle Joseph practically spitting across the table.

"I suspected."

"So did I," Aunt Juliette interjects.

Both of my parents look at Juliette aghast.

"I can't believe I took a chance and trusted you with my daughter this one damn time, and you allow some incestuous bullshit to go on in your own house." My father says. His words laced with venom.

I swear Aunt Juliette's about to cry.

Uncle Joseph slams his hand on the table, stands up, and then Roman also pulls back from the table but still holding onto my hand.

"Don't you ever fucking speak to my wife like that again. These two would have to be related for this to be incestuous, and you and I both know that them being cousins by marriage has nothing to do with this shit. You never thought I was good enough for your sister and you don't think my son is good enough for your daughter. End of story."

"You're damn straight!" My father barks.

"Everyone shut the frack up!" I yell. Roman squeezes my hand tighter.

"I got this, Duchess." he says.

"Not this time," I tell him. "I got it."

"I am twenty-four years old, this is my birthday, and you all are arguing over a moot point. I am with Roman. I love him. That's it. That's all.

Dad, whatever your issues are with the Mastersons has to stop. You've missed years of your only sister's life already, and you may lose some of mine if you keep it up."

"They're murderers, Elizabeth."

"Oh fucking please," Uncle Joseph says.

"Do you know that for a fact or are you holding onto some high school gossip about my father from a million years ago?" Roman asks.

"Do I know for a fact that you've probably buried a couple of bodies in your lifetime and that your father has ten times more than that? No. But I don't need evidence to know the truth."

"Really, because I thought that's what you deal with on a daily basis at your job," my aunt interjects. "Lawyers working hard every day to gather evidence to prove their version of the truth for their clients."

"Juliette," my father responds.

"I miss you," she says. A few tears rolling down her face. "I just want my brother back. Let this go," she pleads.

The silence in the room is deafening.

My father's face looks almost haggard as he considers everything that's just transpired in this dining room. I know he wants to end this. He's just so stubborn.

"I'm sorry, Juliette. I take back what I said about Roman and *him*." He's referring to my uncle. "But I can't cosign this thing between Elizabeth and the boy. I won't."

"That's fine," Roman says curtly. "Lucky for us we're grown, and we don't need anyone's approval."

"We're leaving," my father says to my mother. "Get your things."

My mother doesn't say much. She gives me a long hug, tells me she loves me, and happy birthday. I suppose it's how she's always dealt with my father. How she keeps the peace. He pretty much runs the roost. I'm going to try really hard not to turn out like that.

"Bye, Mom. Bye, Dad." I give my father a brief hug.

"I still love you. I just don't approve of all of your decisions, kiddo."

"Can't we agree to disagree?" I ask.

"Maybe in time. I just can't do it now. Hell, maybe in a month you won't even be with him. Then this would have all been for nothing."

"Maybe, Dad, but I seriously doubt it."

After my parents leave it's time for round two.

"Are you happy now old man?" Roman challenges. "You've ruined Elizabeth's birthday dinner. Is that what you wanted?"

Juliette has been unusually quiet for the last fifteen minutes. I don't like it. I'm not use to it. I don't like that my father has made one of the most positive and loving women I've ever known look like she's just lost her best friend … again.

"I warned your ass. This is your fault. Now you're going to have to find your mother all on your own."

Both Juliette and I whip our heads around.

"What did you say?" she asks my uncle.

"Oh he didn't tell you?" Roman interjects. "He told me

he knows where my mother is, has known for years, and would only tell me if I left Elizabeth alone."

"What," Juliette says in a hushed tone. One dripping in disappointment and sadness. "You knew where his mother was this whole time, Joseph?"

He sighs. "Yes."

"And you failed to mention it to a boy who has been hurting for years over his mother?"

Roman begins to shift back and forth between his feet. This conversation about his mother is making him antsy. I grab his hand again in hopes that it will calm him or at least to let him know that I've got him. Just like he had my back.

"I made a judgment call."

"You made the wrong one," Juliette responds.

"Excuse me you two, but I don't feel well. Happy birthday, Elizabeth. Why don't you go out and try and salvage what has turned out to be one of my greatest dinner party and family reunion failures."

"Julie," Joseph calls out to her as she goes upstairs to the master bedroom and slams the door. He follows her upstairs. I've never seen him move so fast.

"Juliette, open the door."

She doesn't.

I sit and stare at the dinner table full of food, dirty dishes, and desserts and I start to feel a little sorry for myself.

"Happy frackin' birthday to me!" I slam myself down into my chair, cross my arms and sulk. But Roman is standing in front of me with the widest grin on his face.

"What could you possibly be so happy about?" I ask in my pouty voice.

"You love me, Duchess?"

Roman

THE MOST INTERESTING metamorphosis is taking place inside of my body. For once in my life, I'm actually fucking happy. I once believed that happiness was an overrated emotion, one reserved for children and idiots, but I think I know differently now.

Elizabeth makes me happy.

What started out as a lustful attraction in the middle of a club, and then grew into an unexplainable need of possession, is now a full blown wonderful fucking thing that puts a smile on my greedy face every single morning.

Elizabeth: Good morning.

Me: Duchess.

Elizabeth: You haven't called me yet.

See, I'm grinning already.

Me: No I haven't.

Elizabeth: Well what were you waiting for?

Looks like the both of us are getting a little greedy.

Me: I'm calling you now.

* * *

"Finally," she blusters on the phone.

"I literally just cracked my eyes open."

"Well I've been up working for over an hour, and now I want to talk."

I grin to myself.

"What do you want to talk about nerd?"

"I don't know … whatever."

"Juliette hasn't come out of her room yet?"

After Juliette and Joseph argued about him holding back critical details on the whereabouts of my mother, Juliette's been holed up in their bedroom for the last few days while he's been relegated to sleeping in the guest room. I take great pleasure in the old man's temporary pain. Joseph hates to sleep apart from his precious Juliette. Serves him right.

"No, she's surfaced, but now she's never in the house. Always meeting a friend for lunch, going to an exercise class, or meeting someone for this or that fundraiser."

"So basically what you're saying is that you don't have your buddy in the house to talk to, so you're waking me up instead?"

"Am I bothering you?" she asks in a voice laced with irritation.

"Well baby, this would be a whole lot easier if you were right here in this bed with me instead of still over there. Then we could have talked all night and this morning. I mean since you love me and all."

"Oh good grief. Would you shut up about that. I was just trying to make a point that night."

"Oh and you made it loud and clear. I should have recorded it on my phone for posterity; that way we can always remember how adamantly and convincingly you made your point."

"I don't want to talk to you anymore," she grumbles.

I can't help but let out a hearty laugh.

"Why don't you bring your sweet little ass over here, and I'll fix you one of my famous lattes and a bagel. Then we can talk all day if you want."

"You don't have to work?" she asks in a whiny voice.

"Oh stop it. I'll pick you up in thirty minutes, Elizabeth. Be ready with an overnight bag."

"Hey, sexy," I say as Elizabeth slides in the car.

She smiles at me, and I can't help but grab her gently by the neck and pull her in for a good morning kiss.

This is what happy looks like.

"Let's not go back to your house yet," she says. Now I'm curious.

"Why?"

"I want to take you to one of my favorite places today. You showed me the boathouse, and I'm going to show you my place."

"All right where are we headed?"

"Let me drive."

"You can't be serious right now."

"Come on, you never let me drive."

"Because I don't want you crashing the Rover."

"I can drive, Roman."

"You've been taking buses or walking everywhere for the last six years. When's the last time you've driven a car? Let's be honest here."

"Ethan let me drive his car."

It's official. I know that I'm turning into a straight pussy, because a comment like that normally would have set me off. Today I just find it only slightly annoying.

"Ethan almost got you killed, but let's not split hairs," I say.

And then I grab a couple of M&Ms from the center console, make my way around to the passenger seat, and then tell her to, "Drive."

She looks at me for a moment as if she's considering the error of that comment but wisely decides not to address it any further.

"Just sit back and relax. I've got the wheel."

In about fifteen minutes, Elizabeth drives close to Penn's campus to a large playground that's nestled in a West Philadelphia residential neighborhood. It's a pretty big and well-kept city park, with lots of towers to climb, maze-like tunnels, sliding boards, and plenty of swings. Quite the opposite of the only small playground in my old neighborhood where you were lucky if there was even one working swing. Most had been vandalized by the punks and corner boys from the block.

"So this is your favorite place?" I ask as she finds us a parking space on a small side street diagonally across from the park.

"Yep."

"Interesting."

"There's a community center over there in that building. Penn funds several programs in there, and I use to work at one of the student-run computer labs there while I was interning."

"Oh that's cool. Bet the kids loved you."

"It was really cool. Sometimes their time with me was the only time the kids would get a chance to use a computer to finish their homework. I felt really useful there. Then when the day was over, I'd come out here and swing for a while, while I kept an eye on some of the kids who were waiting on their parents to pick them up. There were always a few parents who were late."

"Yeah that's normal for a lot of city kids. Parents work, sometimes they work far and long hours. Public transportation sometimes increases that commute time as well. It's hard for them. I kind of had an advantage over some of those kids though. I learned early never to wait on my mom. I just got myself places and got myself home, and if I couldn't make it happen then I just didn't go."

Elizabeth takes my hand and we walk to a set of swings.

"Push me," she orders.

She looks ridiculously beautiful and almost way too young for me as she swings, hair flying all over the place, a smile on her face so bright that it could give the sun a run for its money.

It's in this moment that I know.

Recognition finally clicks in.

She's it for me.

I love her. I'm in love with Elizabeth Hill.

My cousin.

"You know, Roman, we haven't talked about this whole thing regarding your mother and Joseph. You don't talk about her at all. I don't think it's really healthy."

"Are you a mental health professional now?"

"I'm a Roman Masterson expert and he's certifiable ... so I guess so."

I give her an extra hard push for that smart ass comment.

"Aaah!" she cries out. "Too high."

"I don't like to talk about my mother, Elizabeth."

"I know but that doesn't mean that you shouldn't."

"She left me alone a lot. She was unpredictable. I was a frightened little boy for much of the time, and then I turned into an angry teenager, and now I'm this. I blame her for much of that."

"But in spite of her selfishness and neglect, *this* turned out to be so frackin' magnificent, Roman."

I grab the swing by the sides of her hips and immediately stop it.

"What did you say?" I ask as I step around in front of her.

"I said you're magnificent Masterson, and good or bad, she's still your mother. I'm not saying you need to take her out to dinner and buy her flowers. I'm just saying, find out where she is, and if you want to take it a step further then do it. Go to her. Not for her but for you."

She places a palm on my chest.

"To maybe give some of what's inside here some closure. Some peace."

"You want that for me?"

"Of course I do."

"Because you love me?" I jest.

I pull her close to me and she wraps her legs around my waist.

"Yes, Masterson," she says solemnly. Not backing down from the seriousness of the moment. "Because I love the frack out of you, and I want you to be happy."

I pull her in even tighter and kiss the side of her face while inhaling the scent of Jasmine seeping from her skin. She wraps her arms around my neck, and I lift her completely out of the swing and into my arms.

"I love you too, Duchess." I rumble in her ear.

She pulls back her face and makes my eyes the focal point of her attention. After a brief moment of silence between us a grin spreads across her face.

"I know you do."

28

Elizabeth

"TODAY, Duchess, you've been nothing but a good girl and good girls don't get punished. They get rewarded."

My smile widens with anticipation. This is new territory the two of us are headed in. I can feel it.

While I love my orgasm bully and all of his little torturous bedroom games, I think that I'm going to enjoy this side of Roman too. The side that doesn't feel the need to control every single thing that happens between us sexually and making sure that I'm always orgasm drunk. The side that is sometimes fine with me taking the lead and making sure that he gets what he needs.

I begin with Roman's shirt. A tight fitting dark blue Henley that needs to come off right the frack now, because as soon as it's off I'm going to trace my tongue across all the swirls and curves of the intricate ink on Roman's back.

"That feels amazing, Duchess." He moans while sitting on the edge of the bed as I caress his back, neck and arms with my hands and my mouth.

"Now take off your pants," I order.

He flings open his belt buckle, unzips his jeans, and

does his best to yank them off quickly with me still touching him.

I can already see his heavy erection bulging through his boxers, but right before he moves to slide them down, I stop him.

"Uh-uh. Leave them on for now."

He exhales in a mixture of want, need and frustration. I love it because it makes me feel powerful. Like he really wants me badly; like I'm the only one he'll ever want.

"Do you want me, Masterson?" I ask as I wrap myself around his waist and he holds me steady with both hands under my ass.

"Hell fucking yes."

I slowly tongue kiss him.

"Do you want to fuck me or make love to me?"

"Both."

I giggle then I tongue kiss him again. Making sure to slowly tease him with my mouth the way that he loves so much.

"Which do you want to do first?" I ask.

He stalls for time I think by kissing me around my neck and my cleavage.

"Well?" I ask as I so obviously bend my neck to the side so he can have better access.

His head pops up and looks at me with a serious glare. "I just realized something, baby. Every time I've been with you we've already been making love. I just didn't know it at the time."

I can see he means every single thing he just said. I know it in my heart and my gut, and it makes me feel like the most special woman on the planet.

I have on my very sexy and expensive gift from Roman. My mustard and black lingerie. This time complete with garters. I slip off the tiny lace thong that came with the set and throw it on the floor of Roman's bedroom as I slide somewhat gracefully up the length of his bed on my back. Staring at him the entire time.

I watch as he strokes himself harder and harder through his boxers. He's chomping at the bit. He wants me, but I want him more. He just doesn't know it.

"Will you keep the rest of it on?" he asks very politely with a plea in his eyes that would just be cruel to refuse.

"Of course Masterson. Would that make you happy?"

"Fuck. Yes," he exhales.

"Come here."

Roman obeys but of course puts his own little twist on my orders. He begins by kissing my toes and working himself slowly up my body. Rubbing my calves. Kissing me behind my knees (which tickles by the way).

Kneading my thighs. Kissing me on the sides of my hips. Licking the exposed skin of my waist between the garter belt and my bra over and over until I start panting. Making sure to elicit the reaction he craves. My desperate need for him.

Once he reaches my breasts, I'm drenched, my breaths are heavy and I'm pretty sure the tables have just turned.

"I love this nipple right here because it's so responsive. That puffy areola just pebbled into a tight and taut bundle of nerves as soon as I licked it."

He licks it again.

"See."

His hand moves underneath me and he expertly unhooks my bra. Something he's clearly had a tremendous amount of practice doing, but never the less an image I need to shake clear from my head. He tosses it somewhere in the room and then starts licking and sucking my other breast.

"Spread your legs, Duchess."

I immediately spread my legs apart.

"Wider."

I again follow directions and grow wetter with each passing moment.

"Let me inside baby where I belong. Where I want to stay forever."

And he swiftly thrusts inside of me then slowly slides back out to the tip, then deeply back in again. Again and again as my grip on his back becomes tighter.

"Wider, baby," he pants. "In fact, let's put those legs over my shoulders so you can really feel how much I love your pretty ass."

And deeper he goes.

Eventually sending me into an orgasm oblivion that rocks me to my core.

"I love you," I say in a breathless daze.

"I know you do," he smiles.

We make love again.

This time in a spoon position. His fingers on my clit, rubbing me rhythmically, while he plunges inside me from behind. This time he can't help himself and whispers a few little dirty things to me in my ear. I guess there's something primal about fracking me from behind me that gets my man going.

"You like it when I go in deep don't you, Duchess?"

"Yes, Masterson."

"You like it when I talk to you like this don't you? You tell me to shut up all the time, but I think you're lying. You like this dick all up in you don't you? You want it all the time don't you?"

"Masterson—" I pant.

"See," he laughs. "You like it so much you're about to come all over me right the fuck now aren't you?"

He continues to work in between my legs with his fingers and his cock, and before I know it I come again.

Hard.

Then he follows right behind me. Grunting several unintelligible words.

"You're not a good listener," I say out of breath while he plays with my hair.

"What do you mean?"

"Somehow you turned things around. This was supposed to be my show."

"It was baby. It was all you. You were the producer, the director and the star."

"I don't know, Roman, I feel like I just got bamboozled. My reward was supposed to be me dictating what goes on in the bedroom today."

"And you did. Expertly I might add. I can definitely get use to all of this *making love* we do if the end result is sticky sheets."

"Ugh! You're hopeless."

"Come here."

"No."

He ignores my half-hearted refusal and then lifts me up on top of him.

"There's no better control a woman can have than riding her man. You dictate everything. I just lay back and enjoy the ride if that's what you want."

I sit up while Roman bends his knees with his feet flat on the bed, so that I can use his thighs to lean back on.

"When did you first know you loved me?" I ask him.

"When I saw you on the dance floor of The Lotus. Dancing like nobody was watching."

"I don't believe that."

"It's true," he says while massaging my breasts.

"When did you know you first loved me?" he counters.

"When you flew out to the Bahamas and tried your very best not to kill my ex. Only a man in love would do that." I kid.

"You know what, it doesn't matter when we thought we knew. We know now. I know that I'll never fucking let you go, Duchess. I know that I'll move heaven and earth to make you happy in the bedroom and out. I know that you make me laugh, you inspire me, you motivate me, and you're good for me. There's no doubting that. You were made for me baby."

Tears stream down my face, and why wouldn't they? Masterson is an onion. A man with many layers like he said. And so of course I'd be moved to tears as he peels each layer back for me, one by one, revealing all the wonderful layers of the man that he is.

My man.

29

Elizabeth

AS I STRETCH out like a lazy cat across my bed, I love how my new home is already buzzing with a vibrant energy that I've never experienced before.

Outside there are cars whizzing by, horns beeping without restraint, pedestrians walking with purpose, trucks making deliveries and an assortment of other city centric sounds.

Inside there is just as much energy but of a different sort. Sloan has taken it upon herself to measure and re-measure all of my large, commercial sized windows for window treatments. I love how the sunlight pours into the windows during the day and the moonlight at night, but even I have to admit that it doesn't make for the easiest working conditions during the day. There's glare and distractions; not to mention all the people that can peep inside and take a look at what we're doing on their way to the bus stop ... and do.

I watch from my loft area as she pulls out her heavy duty measuring tape and goes about measuring the width and length of each window, as well as the length of each entire wall. Making sure to jot down her measurements on a small notepad, then worrying that she wrote down the wrong ones for the wrong window, and starting the entire process all over again. All this while Cutter King watches her with the curiosity of a stealth-like cat. I've never seen him this quiet or this calculated before.

It's … interesting.

Sitting at my new dining room table (that I love), which is basically a large slab of reclaimed wood that's been buffed and polished into a smooth shine, are Camden and Jade. I have no idea what those two are talking about down there, but whatever it is has Jade laughing hysterically. Which is not something that I can say I've seen a lot from her. She's always so serious. I think that I like that it's Camden who's putting those smiles and giggles inside of that tiny powerhouse.

I can see from up here that my office is empty, but that the door is open and the office light is on in the second office, which lets me know that Roman is here and working.

It's pretty much his office now.

I ended up not hiring a full-time local coder, but decided it was more cost efficient and made more sense to continue to contract the work out to the most qualified coders wherever they lived. Plus Roman needed some-where to meet and work since he and the King brothers have completely severed business ties with Joseph.

After my birthday fiasco, and Juliette and Joseph's subsequent cold war, they finally made up, and now they're stronger than ever. Of course Joseph had to promise to give Roman his mother's whereabouts as well as give Juli-ette a month long trip to a new continent every year. So

Joseph finally retired, for real this time, and now they're in Egypt touring the Pyramids.

For a variety of reasons I have yet to deeply explore with Roman, he's refused to takeover his father's business. Instead deciding to only take Mendez with him as a client and moving on.

Clearly there is more mending that needs to occur between Roman and Joseph to salvage their relationship, which I am dedicated to make happen. I absolutely want Roman to have some sort of relationship with his parents however surface it may be. I just want as much normal for him as I can manage to create. He deserves it.

My parents are also a work in process. They refuse to come visit me while I'm "playing house" with my cousin, but at least we're talking. My mother has started back texting me about the going ons of the neighbors and my father ... well at least I hear him tell my mother that he said hi during our Sunday phone calls.

Baby steps.

Even though getting our family on board with our relationship has been like pulling some very painful impacted wisdom teeth, the fact that we have the support of our closest friends has been a lifeline. One that I don't take lightly. We're a small little community, the six of us, and I love it.

I especially love the center of it all ... Roman.

"You finally woke up sleepy head?" he asks while climbing the staircase to the loft.

"I stayed up way too late last night."

"Talking to that guy in India instead of what you should have been doing."

"I think we do plenty of that," I grin.

Roman sits on the edge of the bed and swings me around to straddle his lap.

"It can never be too much, Duchess."

"Roman," I whisper. "Not while everyone is in here."

"Glamazon!" Roman turns his head and yells downstairs. "When are you going to do the whole curtain thing up here that we talked about?"

"Calm your tits, Black Knight. I'm on it!" she hollers back. "Damn! You act like you live here."

I giggle because she's right, he does practically live here, although technically he still resides in his penthouse. I needed to have some control.

"You two are absolutely hysterical," I say to him.

"Keep laughing and I'll fuck you right now in front of my friends and yours."

"Shut up. No you wouldn't."

Roman pulls my hips and butt in closer, and I immediately feel just how serious he is right in between my legs.

"Stop it," I whisper again in his ear this time. It's a half-hearted stop though, because I kind of find myself wishing we had some sort of privacy barrier up right now too. There's not a moment that I don't want Roman touching me, kissing me, inside of me.

He pauses for a moment to look into my eyes. Then he grasps a few of my stray hairs in his hand, rubs them between his fingertips, and gently places them behind my ear.

"Are you happy?" he asks me with a fierce intensity that I'm not sure I've ever seen from him before.

I place both of my hands on the sides of his face and use my thumb to gently rub back and forth over his scar.

"Ecstatically, Masterson," I assure him.

Then we kiss passionately, languidly, and without reserve while Mr. Tibbs licks the bottoms of my feet.

I think that I'm finally growing on him.

Ready to find out what happens next? Roman & Elizabeth's journey gets complicated in **Masterson In Love**.

TAP TO DOWNLOAD THE BOOK INSTANTLY!

Masterson In Love

"They all think that I'm a phase. A fetish. A temporary fixture. But I love Elizabeth, and there isn't sh*t anyone can do to change or destroy that … even her."

READ NOW

Dear Reader,

Thank you for reading Masterson Unleashed. I hope you're still enjoying Roman & Elizabeth's story. It was my pleasure to write it. There's something about this couple that will always be near and dear to my heart. I frackin' loved them! Based on reader feedback, I continued my favorite couple's story in the third installment of the series: Masterson In Love.

Also I am a reader first, and an author second, so my goal as an author is to tell stories that readers love. That's why your feedback is critical to me. Please write me at Lisa@LisaLangBlakeney.com or join my private fan group on Facebook at http://facebook.com/groups/romancen injas and tell me your thoughts.

Finally, I need a favor. If you are enjoying the series, I humbly ask that you please leave a review for any or all of the books in the series on the retailer where you purchased it and to please recommend the series to your friends. This

really helps me as an author, as those ratings are so very important to us independent authors and allows other readers to find our books.
xoxo,
Lisa

P.S. Make sure to *Join My VIP Readers List* or my <u>Private Facebook</u> Group to be notified immediately of my next release.

Where You Can Find Me

MY VIP LIST (Get the nitty gritty)
I have a VIP Reader mailing list. I only send free books, new release, sales or special giveaway information to this group. No spam. You can join here:
http://LisaLangBlakeney.com/VIP

MY PRIVATE FAN GROUP (Casual fun)
Join my private Fan Group on Facebook also known as my "Romance Ninja Warriors" where I share all things new going on, celebrate birthdays, post teasers, yummy pics, giveaways and just chit chat.
http://LisaLangBlakeney.com/community

THE ARC TEAM (Book Reviewers)
If you are interested in joining my beta reader team then please join here: https://geni.us/N8jAU

Also From Lisa Lang Blakeney

The Masterson Series
Devour this addictive series about the possessive bad boy,
Roman Masterson, who falls hard and fast for the girl he's
promised his family to protect.
Masterson
Masterson Unleashed
Masterson In Love
Masterson Made
Joseph Loves Juliette
Masterson Box Set

Masterson Next Generation Series
The crazy hot fruit doesn't fall far from the tree. Dive into
this second generation of Masterson men!
Knox - Knox & Gigi
Bronx - Bronx & Karma
Seven - Coming soon!

The King Brothers Series
Dive into this series of interconnected standalones

featuring 3 alpha hot brothers and the women they lay
claim to without apology.
Claimed - Camden & Jade
Indebted - Cutter & Sloan
Broken - Stone & Tiny
Promised - All King Brothers
King Brothers Box Set

The Nighthawk Series

Sexy & sweet sports romances set in the professional world
of football. All standalones.
Saint - Saint & Sabrina
Wolf - Cooper & Ursula
Diesel - Mason & Olivia
Jett - Jett & Adrienne
Rush - Rush & Mia
Freak - Freak & Willow
Brick - coming soon!

Acknowledgments

Do people really read this section? Okay then, I guess I'm starting to realize what it must feel like when an actor wins an Oscar or an Emmy. They know they have to give an acceptance speech and thank everyone, and they're terrified that they're going to forget someone. I'm feeling that right the frack now!

Let me start by saying that I have to thank first and foremost **my family** (hubby and girls) for putting up with my "free for all" dinner nights. Every man for himself so to speak. I want to also thank you for all your enthusiasm in supporting my journey in writing this series even though none of you are going to read them:) Not until you're 40. I also want to thank my extended family members who I finally confessed what I'm doing everyday at the computer to. Thanks for being so supportive and excited for me. It really meant a lot (In-laws, Godmother, sisters, cousins, aunts)!

Thank you to my inner circle of girlfriends. Women who I've known since I was just a kid. Women who have supported everything I've ever done and did once again with the publishing of this series: **Kelly, Donna, Robin, Tracy, Vicki, Erica, Stacey, Kelly J.** Love you all:)

Thanks to my amazing editor **Marla Esposito**, fellow NYU alumnus, and all around amazing woman. Thanks for making my words shine and sparkle!

Thank you to my author mentors: **Liv Morris &**

Jordan Silver who have without a doubt supported me in countless ways during this amazing ride.

Thank you to **Yolanda Ann** of *Art Of Romance*. This woman is really dedicated in a very real way of supporting indie authors and has been so very helpful to me every step of the way. She also helped me break my Facebook cherry:) The good karma that is coming back to you is going to be phenomenal Yolanda!

Thank you to **Ena & Amanda** of *Enticing Journey Book Promotions* and all the book bloggers who have supported me in promoting both Masterson 1 & 2 when it first released as Cousins. I didn't know how on earth new readers were ever going to find my books, and now I understand that a lot of it has to do with the voodoo that you all do!

Shout out to all my amazing **Alpha Romance Warrior Ninjas**, fellow **JS Butterflies** and fellow **VBB Vixens**. You know who you are! I wouldn't be here without any of you. That is for dang sure.

Thank you to all of the **amazing indie authors** I have met so far. Perhaps you purchased my book and liked it, maybe you spread the word about my book to your social media circle, perhaps we did an author takeover together, maybe we even chatted it up casually at some point. In whatever way you've supported me, thank you so very much. As you know, this can be a very lonely profession. It's nice to have some author friends who "get me".

About the Author

Lisa Lang Blakeney is a USA Today Bestselling author of contemporary romance sold in more than 28 countries. Worried that her fellow PTO moms might disapprove, she wrote and published her steamy debut novel Masterson under a different title and pen name in August of 2015.

Thanks to strong reader support of her alpha male character, Roman Masterson, she was encouraged to continue with the series and published the entire Masterson Trilogy the following year. She hasn't looked back since and continues to write novels featuring strong alpha men and the smart women they seek to claim.

A romance junkie for sure, you can find Lisa watching a romantic comedy, reading a romance novel, or writing one of her own most days of the week. If she's not doing that, she's outside in the garden tending to her roses.

Lisa is the wife of one alpha (whom she met in college), mother to four girls, and two labradoodles. Get news on releases, sales and giveaways when you become one of Lisa's VIP readers at : http://LisaLangBlakeney.com/VIP

facebook.com/authorlisalangblakeney

twitter.com/LisaLangWrites

instagram.com/LisaLangBlakeney

amazon.com/author/lisalangblakeney

bookbub.com/authors/lisa-lang-blakeney

goodreads.com/Lisa_Lang_Blakeney

pinterest.com/lisalangwrites

tiktok.com/@lisalangblakeney

patreon.com/lisalangblakeney